SOLÈNE

FRANÇOIS DOMINIQUE

SOLÈNE

Translated from the French by Samuel Martin

OTIS BOOKS

THE MFA WRITING PROGRAM

Otis College of Art and Design

LOS ANGELES █ 2018

© François Dominique
Published originally as *Solène* (French)
(Paris: Verdier, 2011)
English Translation © 2018, Samuel Martin

Book design and typesetting: Olivia Batker Pritzker

ISBN-13: 978-0-9860836-7-9

OTIS BOOKS
THE MFA WRITING PROGRAM
Otis College of Art and Design
9045 Lincoln Boulevard
Los Angeles, CA 90045

https://www.otis.edu/mfa-writing/otis-books
otisbooks@otis.edu

To Frédéric Stochl, musician
To Mike Holland
To Anna Perenna

May the child's voice in him never be silenced, may it fall like a gift from the sky offering to dried-out words the brilliance of his laughter, the salt of his tears, his all-powerful savagery.

— LOUIS-RENÉ DES FORÊTS, *Ostinato*

IT'S HOT OUT; THE CICADAS ARE CREAKING. My brothers are dragging their feet on the gravel. My parents are napping under the magnolia tree. Nik wants a game of see-through-hands or trading-glances. I prefer to go to my room and read with my eyes closed, plugged into my console. We're lucky, the electricity is still working, but it's impossible to communicate beyond the protected zone because of wave interference. On our mirometers there's only a slush of grey dots and a lot of crackling.

I can't seem to concentrate on certain words passing through my mind, even though I love this book, *Anna Perenna* – it was my birthday present. I think about Ludo. Last night, my little brother got up to go to the bathroom. It was stormy out, and a bright flash of lightning flooded the hallway. Ludo came running back to bed, put his head under the covers, and began singing softly. It was beautiful – not that he was aware; it was the song of a frightened child.

Nik and Rob are my older brothers; they share a room on the top floor, to the left of ours. Between these two rooms is our bathroom. A hallway separates the children's side from the parents', which has their bedroom and a washroom, followed by a storage room, my father's study, and the toilet opposite the stairwell. Each end of the hallway is lit by an oval window. The one at the back by my room has tinted panes; it overlooks a shed, a red cedar hedge, and an outer wall.

There's a paved hall at the bottom of the stairs. If you're facing away from the tall oak door at the front, you'll see a glass door leading to the ground floor hallway; on the left is a row of cupboards up to the cellar door; on the right are the kitchen and the living room. Under the roof, there's an attic used as storage space, and a small room with a slanted ceiling where we're not allowed to go...

Our house is called the Borders. It sits on a hill looking out over the ruins of Caluire and La Croix Rousse. It's best not to go wandering around in Caluire; all you see are urns lined up on the doorsteps along the sidewalks, and far too many brambles and nettles. My father says it's the same in Geneva, Trantor, Dunwich, Prague, Opar, Carcosa, Berlin, London, New York, Aman, Rome, or Xanadu, to say nothing of the cities submerged beneath the water...

We live in a zone full of abandoned gardens. In this season, the meadows and fallow fields are covered with wildflowers. Our walls are supposedly shared by other domains. Are the other houses empty? Occupied? I have no idea; it's not advisable to go and find out. The Borders is a stone's throw from the village called Poleymieux, a well-known hideaway for cats, rats, and the Ashen who deserted the ruins of the lower city.

Every morning, my father, who's a doctor but not very handy around the house, fiddles with broken appliances in the hope of catching some piece of news from the outside world. Mother comes up with a project for the day, takes care of the meals, and listens for the hundredth time to her favorite music, Montéclair's cantata. Meanwhile, Ludo and I play behind the house near the shed and the cedar hedge, or else on the steps, while the adults make plans for the future: to repair the mirometers, build lookout cabins in the taller trees, put the provisions in the cellar out of the reach of rodents, revive the vegetable patch at the bottom of the garden...

My father is always claiming we have "substantial" supplies, but for how long? He forbids us to leave the grounds of the Borders. All the same, at dawn one morning I found him by the outer wall, near the red cedars, talking to a neighbor. Again this morning, I saw arms reaching through the branches, without catching sight of a single face. I heard whisperings, the sounds of paper being crumpled around strange bundles.

I'm talking about the morning, but the day has already gone by, I don't quite know how, since the days are alike, and time seems to be contracting bit by bit, unless it's the reverse...

We have supper in the kitchen: gratin of glebas. Nik and Rob argue whether it's possible for an infant to speak as soon as it's born. My father laughs at them, and raises his arms to the sky in exasperation. Then he turns to me. "What do you think, my dear?" I don't have any idea, but one sees all kinds of things... For example, it seems I know how to read other people's thoughts. Was I born like that? It's not for me to say.

Mother sighs and looks at us lovingly. "My poor children!" I get up to go to her, and wrap her in my arms. She has a nice smell of vervain; it grows in our garden. Mother says she rubs her neck and hands with the softest leaves. I like that; tomorrow I'll perfume myself the same way.

✦

If you can hear me, it's because I'll have been dead a long time. Our traces will have been found in the rubble of Poleymieux; from among the ashes – if time hasn't erased everything – the archaeologists will have taken our biochips where all our words and thoughts are recorded.

I pass my hand over my forehead, and at my fingertip I feel the starry little scar behind which lies my memory pearl, embedded in the bone at my birth.

If you can hear me, it's because your engineers will have unwound the thread of my thoughts. But for you, I have no face; I'll only ever be a fossil voice contained in this tiny thing. Right?

Likewise, for me you have neither a face nor a voice, for as I speak, I think you don't exist yet, or that you already don't exist anymore, I don't know how to put it... You're very far away, over there... lost in time.

And what if no one found our traces? When I say *our*, I mean my parents, my three brothers and me. What if time had worn down those traces and made them inaudible? In that case, let's say that my thoughts are flying away, that I'm talking all by myself in front of the Borders, while my parents are calling me to supper.

I've given you a name. I'm not going to tell it to you, it's my secret. I'm not a child anymore, and not a woman yet. I was born in winter, and I only like spring, but the spring we have here, now, protected from the lethal shadows and certain harmful creatures, is a terrible season. I expect in your time such dangers have disappeared.

Do you know that Poleymieux is in the Monts d'Or, above La Croix Rousse and the ruins of Lyon? You know Lyon-la-Neuve; it's northeast of the ruins. That huge city, deserted in turn, borders the Rhône, a European river situated between the Alps and the Massif Central, south of the polders of the Paris Basin, north of the salt lakes of Provence.

I'm not very smart, but I'm "full of words," as my mother says teasingly. I'm quite talkative, just like others have a colossal memory, or else are disheveled, full of tics, or have a third eye, the power to levitate, or premonitory dreams... I'm sure you know what I mean. Are we born like that?

I don't complain, since some aren't as fortunate, like the cruel ferals, the Scarraged, and the Ashen. That's all I can say about that. Anyone who wanted to know more would have to ask my father.

I'd like to imagine you as you really are. What kind of man or woman? Do you look like my mother, my father, my brothers? Or me, if you're a girl my age?

I wish I could travel in time and meet you in your own era; most of all I wish I could see your face. That would make it easier for me to trust you with my innermost thoughts. Sadly, no tunnel exists for passing through time... At least, if such a thing does exist, only you have access to it, for I expect your world is wiser and more knowledgeable than ours.

I think of the time separating us as a deep black chasm, where nothing can be seen except faceless words, swimming in the darkness from one shore, where I am now, to the other where you're listening to me in silence.

I talk alone, but sometimes, talking in my head, I feel like I'm entering somebody else's sleep and then waking up in their head, in the middle of the day. Does that come from you, from your own way of thinking or dreaming? I don't know.

I mean that even if there's only a small chance of this journal of my thoughts ever being found, when words come into my head – here in my room or at the edge of the park – they aren't entirely lost, as a thousand words are lost in the world every second; they're flying words, floating thoughts... They wait for an attentive ear before landing, and *ta-da*... Isn't that what happened just now?

In the morning, when I'm up before the others, I go into the garden and see the fog of thoughts; they don't have names, they don't say where they've come from or who carried them; they're seeking form, seeking life... I see them before the horizon, while the sun is still dim. Shortly after dawn, everything warms up slowly, and the colors, rested by night, reawaken for each of us. That's the time I like best.

In a dream, I saw a horde of words getting lost in the air and returning in tatters... I think of the millions of words erased faster than dust by the wind; I think of all the words that came before me, and all that will come after. I would so like to gather them up, to make a few bouquets with them, before the silence swallows everything – even itself.

From one day to the next, I see these bundles of words reappear in the sky like spoiled clouds, and I reach out to pull sentences away. It's a game and it isn't a game. You mustn't hold it against me, I'm only a child.

✦

The Borders and Poleymieux are on the Croix Rampau road, not far from the mill ruin where a certain Mr. Ampère once lived, the inventor of electromagnetism. The memorial of glass and light that surrounded the mill is partly destroyed.

At the bottom of the garden, I often slip in among the trees and climb to the top of my tall copper beech; from there I contemplate the silvery grey ribbons of the Saône and the Rhône, the white towers of Lyon-la-Neuve, the ruins of the old city, and those of Caluire and La Croix Rousse, overrun with lush vegetation and full of the commotion of birds.

A large meadow extends in front of the house. If you turn your back to the façade and look in the direction of Caluire, you'll see the trees at the end of the garden, the copses, and above all a cedar tree, a linden tree, and my copper beech. On the left, there's the outer wall, some rose bushes, a few hazel trees, and the red cedar hedge. On the right are another wall, a clump of hydrangeas, the magnolia tree, and the entry gate, in front of which is a gravel path leading to the steps of the villa. In front of the house grow a summer lilac (the butterflies' kingdom) and a wisteria as tall as the roof.

My parents like the shade of the magnolia tree. It's their favorite spot. My domain, and Ludo's, is at the bottom of the garden: the shade of the copses, two narrow paths, a tunnel of greenery, a hut made of planks, two logs, a linden tree, and my copper beech. My brother and I spend hours in this place with our treasures. Nik and Rob spend most of their time cooped up in their room; they're trying to repair an old mirometer. In ordinary times they would no doubt have found the Borders a great place to go hiking from, but we're not really on vacation – we're refugees.

In no time at all, everything can change: if the electricity stops, then no more bubble around the houses, no more protection; that's when the starving beasts will come rushing in, like the Scarraged or the Ashen; but we all know it will be worse if we're overtaken by the lethal shadows that destroyed our city.

My parents are frightened, but because of us they don't show it. Nik and Rob think of nothing but escape; they say this refuge is a trap. It's different for Ludo and me since we like to play.

Yesterday, while I was listening to Montéclair's cantata with mother, she said to me, "That voice makes me happy whenever I hear it. I'm going to teach you to sing." That night, I dreamed I had always known how to sing, but that I had lost the knack since the exodus. I told Rob, who sniggered. "It's no good showing off – I know you too well!"

"I know you too well..." That hurts, especially just now, since we're in an unfamiliar situation, and I'm afraid we're all going to end up becoming strangers to one another. "I know you too well" is like a slap in the face; I wish I could tell Rob, but I can't, somehow.

I go up to my room. Outside, my father, seated in the shade of the magnolia tree, is sketching the house in a notebook; with medical precision he jots down a few phrases that I can hear from a distance, for I lean out of the window and concentrate on his face without him seeing me.

Villa, said to date back to the Belle Époque. The roof consists of red tiles and gables of zinc. Two jigsawed finials bear a weather vane and a coat of arms, respectively. Halfway up the slope of the roof, four bull's-eye windows are flanked by vents shaped like fish heads. These windows look onto a garret, a loft, and an attic room. The edge of the roof opens out like a swinging seat at the front of the house, over a corbel arch painted dark red. The support and console beams are decorated with plant patterns painted in green. Under the corbel arch, a stone cornice goes around the building. Lower down, on the lintels of the top floor and the ground floor, you can see garlands of dark red and almond-green ceramic, whose color has faded with time. The angles of the building, the borders of the windows, and the front door, as well the balusters and the front steps, are of white stone. The façades have lost some of their yellow roughcast, exposing red bricks here and there.

Honestly, what's the point of describing this house in such minute detail? Aren't there more urgent things to do for our protection? I don't understand my father sometimes, but he does know a lot.

Ludo's calling me. He's found a "baby bunny" lying dead under a thicket. I teach him the word *kit* and other names for young animals. He turns the body over with a stick and asks who killed it. It's the first time he's seen a dead rabbit; he's trembling slightly. I give him a hug and tell him we're going to bury the kit. We dig a grave under a bush, place the animal in the hole, cover it with earth, and decorate with pebbles, soil, and moss. I don't believe this little body will rest in peace for long, for I already see glamurae, carlinews, and red ants getting busy in its stomach. That's life, as my father would say.

Suppertime comes around. Mother makes biscuits. We're seated in a circle around the kitchen table; Daddy sums up the main instructions for our safety and protection. He insists that we're not to leave the Borders, answer the door, or use any appliances, given that the current cuts out at least ten times a day and that our generator only just suffices to maintain the bubble around the property. We listen to the instructions in silence. Ludo whispers to me, asking for explanations.

◆

In certain places, at certain hours of the day, the shadows get busy and slowly destroy whatever they touch.

Well before the exodus, it was thought the residents were suffering from skin diseases. It would begin with red blotches that disappeared overnight, but greyish traces remained on people's skin as if they'd been hit. There wasn't any pain, but they would become thinner and wither away before your eyes; in the end they would disintegrate like clay dolls.

The residents weren't even buried anymore; they were piled up on the embankments. Luckily for us, the refugees are sheltered from the scourge, for they remain in the protected zones.

It's easy to predict the moment when the lethal shadows spread: always in the evening, when the weather's fair, as soon as the sun drops toward the horizon and the light becomes dark red.

When I climb my tree, I can see how the scourge is advancing not far from here. People used to say "shadow sickness," because the walls, plants, animals and humans would be progressively contaminated, before dusk, when they found themselves in shadow; first the walls, crumbling on the east-side façades; then the bark of the trees, peeling away in strips on the same east and southeast side; then the meadows and gardens, yellowed and dried out.

The animals and men were affected after the plants and objects. Obviously, when the animals have bruises, it doesn't show on account of their fur, but they start to tremble, and then they fall, dying of exhaustion, disintegrating on the side of the paths and in the streets where they'd thought to find refuge among men.

Many animals and men broke up like ordinary clumps of earth before the protections were installed.

This is what it's come to! How long will the protections be effective? You're the only one to know, for if you're listening to me right now, it's because you belong to the line of survivors, right?

"Shadow sickness"? It's all very well saying that; nothing harmful happens during the night, but late in the afternoon, especially when the sky is very clear, the dark red light looms as soon as the sun touches the horizon and the shadows lengthen. That's when the objects and living beings previously stricken continue to get eaten away, bit by bit. They end up disintegrating like sand.

This is why at first, the people of Lyon (like those of several world cities, for that matter) had gotten into the habit of going down into their cellars in the middle of the afternoon and not coming out until after nightfall. But this measure isn't enough to save the residents from the disaster, for the apartment buildings, the plants, and all the things that usually make it possible to live during the daytime keep deteriorating. This widespread decay has terrible consequences: the ruin of roofs and walls results in pipes and cables breaking, which in turn results in fires, collapses, floods, and then still more fires, more collapses, more floods. In the end, even the charred ruins are devoured by the lethal shadows, and nothing remains save large black puddles and a dry, white, odorless powder blown by the wind.

For my part, I'd say "light sickness" instead, since it only happens during the day, at the point when the sun goes down. Light sickness: the shadows are outlined by rays of light when they encounter an obstacle, as we all know.

Most of the time, the sun is a blessing. My father could go on about it for a long time: the sun brings life, colors things, nourishes the plants, delights the eye, and warms the atmosphere... So if it's so great, why would the sun bring death among its shadows? I don't know, and neither do my parents.

Here and there, some cities rebuild themselves in the

protective bubbles, but for how long? My parents are very worried, but not me; I'm wild with curiosity... for I was born after the disaster, and when I climb my copper beech, when I look at Caluire, La Croix Rousse, Lyon-la-Neuve, I can't help admiring this mix of ruins, sand, ashes, new vegetation, glass columns in the new city, iridescent globes like soap bubbles. And when it's nice out, when the sun is shining, the light entrances me, and I look forward to this happiness every day, early in the morning, and again tomorrow, and tomorrow, and tomorrow...

I love getting up at dawn; everyone is asleep in the Borders, the birds awaken, and I look for the slightest details with my owl-sharp eyes. The grass in the big meadow is covered with dew.

✦

This morning I hear my parents whispering in the living room. They're wondering what will become of us. My father says he has no idea, but that they'll both "act like" we were on a long vacation, so as not to worry us children.

No matter how softly they speak, they know I listen to their thoughts. Don't worry, dear Mother and Daddy, I'm not afraid... What's going to happen? I'm like an animal on the lookout, hiding under a bush... It's your own fear that frightens me, but I won't tell my brothers; for that matter, Nik and Rob wouldn't listen to me, since they think I meddle in things that aren't my business. As for my dear Ludo, have no fear – I'm protecting him.

Sometimes I need to be by myself, otherwise I think my head would explode. For instance, I linger at the bottom of the garden between the trees. And there, when I'm really alone, the last thing I want is to answer my parents or my brothers if they're calling me; I look around attentively, I observe certain interesting details – and I feel a strange wellbeing.

Under the bushes I see tiny things that only an owl would see at night from a distance; I hear insects nibbling and young birds chirping; I smell the leaves, the moss, the earth: these smells intoxicate me; the colors become brighter, the greens turn to blue, the browns turn to dark red, and the greys turn to yellow: as soon as I move my head, the nuances change; my gaze passes like a paintbrush over gravel, trees, and sky. My heart beats faster, and I could faint, but in fact I'm transported by a feeling of happiness that erases the sadness of the world.

The heat hasn't stopped rising since noon. I say *morning, noon, night*. Time can occasionally pass quicker than my thoughts. It's easy to tell day from night, the beginning of the day from the end, but we've lost the dates and even the names of days since the optical clocks broke down.

In a drawer, my father found an old watch that he can't manage to repair. It's beautiful – it looks like a round seashell of silver and gold. We can't do without time, but how to keep track of it?

My father tries to keep a handle on time in a notebook containing a few reference points: our arrival at the Borders, the end of communications, and the disappearance of images on the mirometers. The same notebook is used to keep track of our provisions and predict the maintaining of the protections without outside help. I imagine that millions of families are doing the same (I mean the families with a shelter from the scourge).

✦

Knocking on the gate of the villa! My father asks Nik to look cautiously through the spyhole in the hall. Nik cries, "It's Rob! It's Rob!" My father races out to the gravel path, opens the gate, seizes Rob by the hand, makes a sweeping gesture in the air for Nik to put the protection back in place, brings Rob into the living room, and bends over him. "There's blood everywhere! But who could have done this to you, my poor boy?"

We're gathered around Rob. A cut on his right temple, another on his right cheek, another under his chin! The blood is flowing, and since he's tried to wipe it away with his sleeve, he's got some on his nose and mouth, his hands, his clothes. My mother turns white, and can't think what to do. My father brings his medical kit, disinfects the cuts, gives my brother an injection, and applies stitches to his face; Rob doesn't cry.

Mother says again and again that we must never leave the Borders, at least not until the situation has improved.

"Who hurt you, poor darling? An animal? A man?"

"A boy my age," my brother stammers.

"How's that possible? With a knife?"

"No, he bit me."

"Like a dog, like a rat?"

"Yeah, like a rat... let go, you're suffocating me!"

Nik tries to reassure Mother. "It's not that serious... you know what the Scarraged get up to; everyone avoids them, they're just sick." My father shakes his head. "You mustn't leave here!" Rob acts all proud; he says he fended off the Scarraged one who bit him; he claims to have broken his nose before running away, before the others arrived. Then he turns to me. "It didn't even hurt!"

Nik stamps his foot and mutters, "If the Scarraged figure out there's a doctor in this house, four walls, a gate and protections aren't going to keep them back!" Daddy sends Rob to his room so he can rest, and maybe to punish him. I ask him what would have happened to Rob if he hadn't been given an injection.

"In that case, Rob could lose his sight, his hearing, and his sense of smell and touch."

"But can you live like that a long time?"

He says no – that people who get bitten, when they're infected, soon lose their speech and can die in their sleep. I ask him if the Scarraged bite each other; he says yes, and immediately adds, "That's why those tribes will gradually die out."

Walking in the meadow, I mull all this over. Ludo follows, harrying me with questions; I ask him to be quiet, to let me think. I imagine myself no longer seeing, feeling, or hearing anything, gibbering like a toad hypnotized by a grass snake. It makes me want to cry. I really don't want to go wandering in the lanes of Poleymieux or the Monts d'Or.

At the time of the exodus, those who were mechanized flew far away from here, but I'm not sure they're any better off than us in the other countries of the world.

✦

Since the biting episode, my father reckons he has to keep his children distracted by any means. He's constantly saying, "Play! Play!" – as if games were the best protection against all danger. I think he's right, in a way – but then what game would we have to invent in order to be truly saved?

This morning, he gathers us together and declares delightedly, "Have a seat around the garden table." Rob, Ludo and I don't need a second invitation; Nik joins us, dragging his feet. My father explains the rules of the game: he proposes that each person in turn give the name of an animal, and that the others have to name that animal's call. The one who wins will be able to choose a prize.

My father starts. "What does the cat do?"

"It meows, Daddy," answers Ludo, jumping up from his chair.

Rob shrugs his shoulders. "Too easy! But once we get to the vulture, or the gallipon... Ludo and Solène will be lost."

"You're forgetting that your sister has all the words," my father says.

"I know! She goes poking around in other people's thoughts, too!" Mother comes to my defense, and decides to be on Ludo's team to even things out.

My father continues. "The eagle?"

"It flies," answers Ludo. Nik laughs at him, and is told to be quiet. Mother raises Ludo's right hand and says in his place, "The eagle shrieks or screams." Daddy is enchanted; we go through all the birds, and I score points without drawing too much attention. Rob's mind is elsewhere; he only comes up with the lark, which *warbles*... But I could have told you, if I hadn't wanted to let Mother and Ludo win, which birds *cackle, whistle, honk, squawk*... which other ones *mew, croak, winnow, hoot, coo*... and you would tell me what *cheeps, chatters, twitters, trills*, or *caws*. This can go on a long time, for since the disaster, thousands of flying species have appeared; they know how to protect themselves from the shadows; their names and the names of their calls, in all the world's languages, form myriads of words that would make your head buzz if you heard them... or make it spin like the weather vane that's creaking right now on the roof of the house!

I watch Daddy out of the corner of my eye, and he watches me the same way. He knows that I know he's afraid. I'm worried the game is petering out. My mother thinks it's over, and tells Ludo, "Come on, we're going to make a birberry pie." My father protests – "No, we haven't finished!" – and leads us into the living room, for it's begun to rain. This time he suggests we play *Chinese portraits*. Nik sniggers and pulls a face. My father shrugs, and announces enthusiastically, "Here are the ancient rules!"

According to these ancient rules, each person has to think

of a human being, an animal, a plant, or a thing. Once they've thought of a word, they have to keep it secret. Then the others ask questions. The one who guesses the word wins. I'm on a team with Ludo, who hasn't completely understood.

The game goes pretty well at first. Ludo thinks of *mother*, which Rob guesses. Rob, in turn, comes up with *bite*, guessed by my mother, who comes up with *caterpillar*... but nobody guesses it. Nik comes up with *blaze*, and we guess *fire*, but it's not the right word. There's a short argument to decide whether we're allowing synonyms.

In the evening, after consuming the same old plate of dried seaweed in silence, Rob confides in me. "You know, I didn't tell the whole story... The day of the bite, I heard what a survivor from Caluire was saying."

"And what was he saying that was so serious, since you kept it from us?"

"He was saying that processions of children are marching very far from here, toward the sea. I think it's a trick to get us to march north in columns with no defense. What do you think? What if it's true?"

Personally, I think Rob didn't say anything because he's too keen to leave here with Nik, to join the processions, to try his luck elsewhere. If he'd let on what he's just told me, my father would have given a speech about the instructions and kept a close eye on him from then on.

I'm sitting in the living room; the light is waning, and the lamps flicker and crackle. Suddenly the light becomes a dirty yellow; my father goes to get his bird calls, and whistles several times; he opens the windows in the living room and the kitchen, and whistles once more in order for the sound to carry. Not long after, fluorescent dragonflies come pouring in from the flatlands and the ponds; they land everywhere, even on Ludo's head, and give us enough light to finish the evening comfortably without having to stumble around in the dark. These dragonflies will leave again at dawn, come the first rays of light. Tomorrow we'll find a few of them motionless on the living room carpet. It's like that whenever they come.

✦

I wake up drenched in sweat. I'm not sleepy anymore. The white light of the moon passes through the shutter cracks. I get up and tiptoe through the hall toward the skylight above the stairwell. I lean forward and look closely: there's the magnolia tree, there are the gravel paths, the copses, the outer wall, the gate. Suddenly, hundreds of bees swarm in front of the skylight and are bumping crazily against the pane. Pressing my mouth to the cold glass, I talk to them. I tell them not to be frightened, to return to their hive. I hear the buzzing of their wings. The pane vibrates, and it tickles my lips. They keep bumping and bumping and coming back again in even greater numbers to the spot where my mouth is pressed to the stained glass. Their calls are humming in my head, but I can't understand them. What do they want? What can sleepless bees ask of a girl wide awake?

At the bottom of the garden I see the leaves, the pebbles, and the tiny creatures scuttling through the grass; my gaze enlarges them like a magnifying glass. Everything is whiter under the full moon.

I leave the skylight and the landing, and hop up and down on the stairs to get rid of cramps. Now I'm on the floor in the entryway. The tiles are cool beneath my feet. I open the tall door and slide up against the balustrade along the steps; I look up toward the skylight: the bees have gone. The black sky flickers with summer lightning. I close my eyes, one finger on each eyelid. I see specks of yellow light. I open my eyes; orange lumps are still sticking to the sky. I rub my eyes; everything becomes black again, and the moon is hidden. Not a breath of air. I can feel a tingling in my mouth and stomach.

A faint irritating noise, like a door groaning on its hinges, comes at me through the silence. I'd better return to my room. Climbing the staircase, I feel like the steps are creaking behind me. The vases are clinking together on the pedestal table. The prints are moving on the walls.

✦

This morning my father asks if we want to play *Chinese portraits* again. No answer. He encourages us by declaring that the winner can help him make coypu skewers for lunch (Nik and Rob caught three last night by the edge of the pond).

The family is seated in a circle in the big meadow. "The youngest starts!" My mother turns to Ludo, and says, "Go on, angel, think of a human being, an animal, a plant or a thing, but don't tell anyone except me, since we're a team." Ludo grips Mother's shoulder and whispers a few words in her ear, taking care to conceal his mouth between cupped hands. He watches us out of the corner of his eye. "You're not allowed to listen or look at me! You're cheating, it's not fair!"

"What a dummy," says Rob. "Just because we're looking at you doesn't mean we can hear you!"

"Dummy yourself!"

And the argument continues, thanks to a bad joke from Nik. Ludo sighs, and again cups his hands to his mouth and whispers in Mother's ear. She squeezes her eyes shut; Ludo's breath and lips tickle. She scratches her ear and shifts away gently. "All right, got it!" Then my father says we have to take turns asking questions, from left to right, or east to west, which amounts to the same thing given our seating arrangement on the grass.

"Rob, your turn to guess!"

"Man or woman?"

"No. Your turn, Solène."

"Animal?"

"Yes, animal," Ludo answers.

Nik sniggers. "Feathery or furry?"

"Hold it," my father says. "We have to ask the questions differently, so that you can only answer with yes or no."

"A furry animal, then?"

"Yes," says Ludo.

"Do you eat it?"

"Don't say that! I won't let you say that!" cries Ludo, who gets up, red with anger.

"Settle down," my father says. "Ludo, your brother is only asking if it *could* be eaten: in other words, if this animal is edible, to hunters, for example..."

"No, no, you shouldn't ever eat it anymore!"

"Never mind, we've got it, it's the galabry, a sweet little galabry... I swear, if I find one in the garden, it's going straight on the spit, and you'll be only too glad to eat it."

"That's not true! I'll never eat one!"

Mother smiles, and observes softly, "Poor children, the galabries disappeared a long time ago..."

Now that Rob has guessed *galabry*, it's his turn to come up with another word, and my turn to ask a question. The game continues. I ask if it's a human being; Robin says yes. Ludo asks if it's an adult; Robin says no, so I say *child*; the answer's yes. "A girl?" Nik asks. The answer's no. My father says *boy*, and the answer's no; Ludo stands and puts his hand up. "That doesn't exist, or else it's a baby that hasn't been born yet!" Saying this, he turns to my mother and blushes. She bursts out laughing, and says she doesn't have any children aside from the four of us.

It's my turn. Suddenly I have a terrible migraine, my vision blurs, I see a swarm of transparent bees; the landscape dances before my eyes; I can't hear; I smell a strong scent of honey and burnt wood, and a word rushes to my lips: "It's the *lam... lim... lumi...*" Before I can get the entire word out – a word I know nothing about, in fact, a word that's passing through my mind – my mother rises, clamps a hand to my mouth, and cries out. My father, quite pale, declares in a grave voice, "Don't ever say that again, Solène! Never again, do you hear? Do you want to be the death of your mother, dammit?!" I'm certain that Rob came up with this word, just to get me to read his thoughts and say it in his place. He avoids my eyes, which makes me sad. I comfort Mother and ask her to forgive me. Ludo is going back and forth between us, asking, "What's going on? What's the word that made Mother cry?" My father tells him to be quiet and asks us all to go play somewhere else; my parents hold each other for a long time before turning back to the house. Ludo follows them, asking, "What's the word? What's the word?"

I hide behind a bush. Nik sees me, and comes up to stroke my hair. "Don't get upset, Solène. Mother and Daddy are worried; we haven't lived through all that they have. Daddy suspects you're ferreting around in his most private thoughts; he'd like to talk to you, but he's not quite sure how. Come on, silly, stop crying, he adores you!"

Nik dries my tears, gives me a kiss and says I should come to lunch. The wild scent of the skewers on the grill makes me hungry. Mother has laid the table in front of the house; she's smiling as if nothing's happened. My father says cheerily, "It's done, children! This will be delicious. Everyone to the table! I'll bring in the beast!"

✦

What a strange noise! It's coming from my parents' room. I go closer and look through the keyhole: my father, his chest bare, is getting ready to slip a nightshirt on. His back is turned to me, but I can still see his face in the bedroom mirror; his movements seem suspended, frozen in the air. He's put his right arm through the sleeve; in his left hand he holds the other sleeve waist-high. He sees his motionless reflection in the glass; he doesn't know I'm observing him. The tall mirror is cracked, but the shards remain gathered around two shining points, the marks of two projectiles from who knows where. The walls and windows are vibrating, the floor as well.

In the mirror, my father's face and body are cut up into fragments. The left ear is higher than the right, and the eye and nose practically blend together. The left arm is in three parts, the stomach in slivers. Poor Daddy. I think to myself that if he makes a single movement, the fragments of glass will suddenly fall.

My father takes a step forward and puts his shirt on quickly; a sleeve touches the surface of the mirror; all traces of a crack disappear. I can now only see the image of the door in the mirror, caressed by the light of day; I can also see the keyhole, the small dark point from which my invisible eye is watching the scene.

I make it back to my room before Daddy emerges from his. I wait a few moments before slipping into the hallway once more, my heart pounding; then, without a sound, I enter my parents' bedroom where the scent of vervain hangs in the air.

My turn to gaze at the tall mirror and the wardrobe! I can see myself entirely, smiling – and not in a thousand pieces! I'm now standing by the first window, to the left of the wardrobe; I can observe enormous blue clouds rolling toward the valley from the Monts d'Or. Will they scatter, or burst? The wind shifts and pushes them back to the north, but they come again, blacker and more menacing. The wind is dropping; they're descending toward the ruins of Lyon. No lightning, no thunder – just the heavy clouds banking up.

I must have fallen asleep for a moment, with my elbows on the window ledge. At the edge of the meadow below, Ludo is making a snail shape with pebbles. Before joining him, I have a sudden idea; I leave the room and tiptoe through the hallway toward my father's study. I stop not far from the door and press my ear to the partition, shutting my eyes. Words crackle in my head. The sweat runs down my forehead and cheeks. My father's thoughts go through me like arrows, and they hurt.

I'm worried about Solène. Her words are not and have never been those of a child. Sometimes I think she's scheming... Nothing surprises her, she always knows in advance what she's dealing with; sometimes her calmness is strange. I should talk to her, but it's difficult – she acts as though she were constantly watching out for my mistakes. I feel I'm being spied on by the child I love most... How many times, looking at one another face to face, have we remained silent? I often see her murmuring something to herself; she furrows her eyebrows, moves her lips, sighs, and nods or shakes her head to approve or disapprove I don't know what. That alone would be enough to worry me, but there's more! In the very moment when I'm watching her, I feel that she's deliberately trying to read my thoughts. She pretends not to see me, and checks that I'm still there out of the corner of her eye. I even imagine that the words and phrases she mutters haltingly in her corner are the very ones I'm thinking of as I watch her. We occasionally exchange knowing looks, but what good does that do, since I can't manage to say what I'm burning to tell her, here and now? For that matter, is she not following the thread of my thoughts from a distance at this very moment, in her hiding place at the bottom of the garden? Solène! Solène! You're really worrying me.

I go downstairs with an ache in my heart. Why doesn't my father speak to me, if he loves me so much? Why doesn't he trust me? Is it my fault if I capture thoughts that aren't my own? I'm made like that, the same way I have tangled brown hair, skin that's too pale, and narrow shoulders, the same way I'm a lousy runner. That's just how it is, I can't help it.

Now I'm playing at the bottom of the garden. My father has left his study. He's in the meadow, walking toward me. "That's it," I think, "he's going to make up his mind!" Now he's only a step away; he reaches a hand toward my face, without touching me. I turn slowly and pretend to look away, while my right hand, clutching a green racket, continues to bounce a red ball attached to the handle with red elastic against the trunk of my tree.

My father could bend down and say something trite, like, "Are you having fun?" – but his outstretched arm falls back heavily at his side; he sighs, discouraged, and turns to walk toward the magnolia tree without giving me any sign. As he leaves, I can't stop thinking, "Give me a kiss. Please."

My father is back in his study, and there, rather than working on what promises to be his Invention, he continues to think sadly about me.

Her face is very beautiful, and sometimes ugly, asymmetrical: this can be seen when she's not moving. Is it because of her right eye, which is smaller than the other? Her crooked mouth? The dimple on her left cheek? The uneven hairline above her forehead? I'm enchanted by the sound of her voice, and by her movements, whether graceful or clumsy. But why does she persist in endangering us with certain words and thoughts? I sometimes think she has us at her mercy. Ah – to have someone at your mercy! That's exactly the sort of phrase she might say, as if it were a game… not to mention the words she doesn't say, busy as she is catching everyone else's; the terrible words that escape her… Who is this child? Solène is my daughter, but I barely know her.

✦

We're all in the living room, seated around a game of patience. There are silhouettes in the middle of it, a bust, a head… a face, no doubt, but what face? We don't know. The pieces of the puzzle are put together, except in the spot where the face should be. Ever since the first day, all our efforts to give the head an appearance have failed. The unfinished form is still there, spread out on the round table in the living room, and my family – whether in the morning, like today, or at night – approaches the table and tries in vain to picture the missing face.

According to my father, there's no solution: the remaining pieces come from another puzzle, whereas the ones we need have been lost. Nik is of a different opinion. Several times, he's taken the pieces apart and put them back together from scratch, convinced that each piece has two or even three different positions, and that we have to look for another image, other silhouettes, other heads, or else neither heads nor silhouettes, but rather a landscape, a boat, and snow-covered shores. I sit next to him, leaning over his shoulder, and listen to him repeat, "Landscape... lake... snow-covered shores..." This sounds vaguely familiar. Maybe a memory from before the exodus, before leaving Lyon-la-Neuve.

I watch the changing sky through the window. Dark clouds blanket it, sped by the wind; they tumble over one another and pile up, turning black. Thunder rolls in the distance, getting nearer. Nik asks Rob to turn the light on; the lamps flicker, and the light trembles.

The air becomes stifling. Lightning crashes. We're by the windows, watching the spectacle of the storm... A thick curtain of rain beats down on the flatlands; it advances on us rapidly, and hides the bottom of the garden altogether. The drumming of the rain, the flashes of lightning and the cracks of thunder are joined by a succession of muffled sounds. Mother says it's hail, but on the meadow and the gravel path we can see small objects falling; they aren't hailstones, more like soft oblong things the size of plums or eyes. You might also call them bubbles. They pile up, quivering, but don't burst.

My father, his faced pressed to the window, grows pale.

"Incredible!" he stammers. "How is it possible that...? And for what...?" The rain and the false hail stop as quickly as they'd started; the clouds drift apart to let the sunlight through at last. The grass and bushes are steaming. Now I can clearly see these soft translucent things; they look like crystal pebbles, but neither glass nor stone have this strange softness. They're flaccid, trembling in the bright light. Their surface is limpid and smooth. The pebble-bubbles gleam in the sun.

Ludo, beside himself, cries, "Bubbles! Lots of them! Let's gather them up, I want to touch them!" My father forbids us to go into the garden. He frowns, scratches his chin, and takes up his observation post once more beside a window. He speaks very softly; his words crackle in my head: *Carnified pebbles... monadelles... monstrances... undulophors... alpha lanterns... girandoles... photobions... ideolabes... pure morphites... let's see, let's see...* But suddenly he raises his arms in excitement, happy to be able to put a name to his discovery, and exclaims in a loud voice, "Ah! Ideoplasts... ambulatory wonders!"

I shut my eyes and grit my teeth. A burning thought forces other words into in my mouth: *Lam... lim... lumi...* I bite my lip until it bleeds, so as not to utter the words. I start to sway; there's a buzzing of bees in my head. Farewell, I'm going... and I...

Mother is bending over me; she passes a moistened towel delicately over my face and makes me drink vervain syrup. "Come back to us, Solène! Come back, sweetheart. She fainted... Oh, how warm you are! It's the fever... don't worry, my dear, those things are all gone."

"Gone! Exactly!" adds Ludo. "I told you they were bubbles, I knew it!"

I turn to Daddy, and say in a weak voice, "The ambassadors..."

"What do you mean by that, Solène? What are you talking about?"

"Yes... ambassadors."

My father looks at all of us, very worried, and then speaks to me as if I'd lost my senses. "Calm down, child..." I walk unsteadily to the window and look out at the garden. The soft pebbles haven't entirely disappeared, but have melted in the sun; whitish water trickles and evaporates; strips of translucent surfaces still cling to the grass. A smell of flint and red ants spreads through the air and reaches us. Rob lifts his nose and sniffs. "Smells like something's burning!"

✦

Nik and Rob have shut themselves in their room. I can enter if I knock three times, but for the moment it won't be necessary. I sketch birds on notebook paper in the living room below, and in my head I can easily hear what my brothers are plotting.

Nik is trying to repair his mirometer. He says we'll soon be obliged to live without electricity, but that the screen can work without it, provided it's modified... I don't know anything about technology; it's my older brothers' passion.

"I've got a funny-looking portrait," announces Nik.

Rob couldn't care less. "What good do you expect that'll do us?"

Their bedroom is full of wires, antennae, outlets, and other fairly ugly contrivances. If I had to sleep there, I would be afraid of making the slightest movement and unplugging everything accidentally, or hurting myself.

"Oh! Who is it?" asks Rob, who has probably turned round to look at the screen.

"It doesn't have a name..."

"Even so, it's really beautiful." I imagine my brothers are bent over the mirometer screen.

"Rob, swear you won't tell anyone!"

"Not even Solène?"

"Not even Solène. We're wrong to think she listens to our thoughts; I reckon she only pretends to, just to draw attention. Don't tell anyone what you've seen, swear to me!"

"I swear on the head of you-know-who..."

"Shush, you fool!"

"I didn't say the word. I'll swear on the head of our mother, if you want. You can trust me."

Silence. Now what are they doing? I'm not sure. What is this mysterious portrait? A bit later, the light flickers and crackles. The light bulbs in the hallway burst. I can hear my father grumbling as he picks up the pieces of glass. I won't tell on my brothers, but if you ask me, it's their fault.

I put my drawing book away and look absentmindedly at the wall between the two windows in the living room. Under a stuffed galabry's head is a framed photo: you can see my parents with their arms around each other at the edge of a great lake, I don't know where – in the mountains, Europe, World. I surely wasn't born; they didn't have any children yet; they look like a young couple soon to be married, in the old way. Why have we never spoken about this beautiful photo, almost certainly taken at the end of the good times? If my parents kept it after the disaster, it must be important to them. You have to talk to children about the past, right? That's what I think, anyway. I'll ask Mother to tell us about that lake and those mountains at breakfast tomorrow.

Mother passes behind me, strokes the back of my neck, takes the vase of flowers from the table, removes the bouquet of white gelinas picked near the pond, discards the wilted flowers, changes the water, and clips the stems.

✦

Ludo claims I'm thinking too hard. We're at the bottom of the garden. He brushes and rebrushes my hair with a bone comb, taking care with my stray locks so as not to hurt me. The friction of the comb makes invisible sparks crackle in my hair. "Stop moving your head, Solène! Keep still!" My eyes roam ceaselessly, and my gaze catches everything that presents itself before me. I observe the return of the redwings and the nuthatches on the branches of my tree; these two species have escaped the devouring shadows.

Many birds come to our place to take shelter, but how do they manage to cross the barrier without tearing their wings? I'd very much like to know. My father says it depends on the angle and speed of their flight. He also says that if we could see what's at the base of the invisible barriers protecting us, on the dry ground we'd find powdered bones and the grey dust of hundreds of insects, along with withered birds and the remains of lemures, cave-dwelling dogs, and other species unable to mutate or adapt. All those poor animals were crushed against the barrier, and lie there for a few days, or a few hours, until the shadows break them up and the wind carries them away.

Oh dear, it's starting to rain. Gigantic, warm drops. They run down my face; I drink them delightedly. "Stop, Ludo, there isn't time to comb my hair anymore – we're soaked through!" He cackles with laughter and carries on as if nothing were happening...

From their windows in the living room and the kitchen, Daddy and Mother gesticulate vigorously, insisting, "Solène! Ludo! Quick, inside!" The rain is so thick that our parents appear very far away, like animated figurines behind a veil.

At last I obey; I take Ludo by the hand, and together we run as fast as we can under the pounding rain. Mother is waiting for us on the steps to wrap us in dry towels, and tells us to hurry on up to our room. "Go get changed before supper!"

At the end of the meal, my father is watching me fixedly out of the corner of his eye. As I see it, his look means, "Stop reading my thoughts, you insolent girl, since I don't read yours! It's impolite!" But at the same time, he's telling himself he adores me; in thought, I reply that I love him too, hoping that for once this kind message will get through to him.

Rob and Mother get up from the table. They go to the living room and bend over the puzzle. "Hooray!" Rob says suddenly. For at the edge of the absent face, he's succeeded in placing one of the pieces that remain.

✦

It's dawn. Mother paces on the landing, jangling her keys. What is she looking for in the storage cupboard? She goes up to the attic and treads around above my head. I'm not tired anymore. Ludo is talking in his sleep, saying, "No, no, don't go there..." I think about the day ahead.

Never knowing what might happen from one day to the next... Isn't that strange? I imagine a giant curtain between *now* and *in a little while*... No, more like a thin veil that I keep brushing against, without being able to reach it. A veil, or else a living skin, as thin as onion peel... This veil or skin is translucent, and yet it's impossible to see what's on the other side – what lies before us, I mean, in a little while; we go forward... we go forward from one instant to the next, it's always now, now...

But time passes; we inadvertently pierce the veil with a sudden movement, and see things as they present themselves; a new landscape, for instance, at a bend in the road... But another veil instantly forms, and then another, and still another; we'll never know where the edge of the future lies. We walk through time with our eyes covered, like in blind man's buff. I know what I'm trying to say, at least – but isn't it rather troubling?

We're bound for fine tomorrows, said the daily messages on the mirometer screens, before the exodus. I should very much like to talk about that with a person who had lived through fine tomorrows – like you, for instance, if you exist... if you hear me... at this precise moment.

No, no... It bothers me to tell of my life in silence, talking all by myself, confiding in this inanimate thing lodged inside me, a tiny natal graft... nothing more than an invisible chip on each person's forehead...

I feel myself becoming a simple marionette, but who pulls the strings? Who makes me speak? It's not my parents, nor my brothers. They could be asking themselves the same questions I am – at least I suppose so, for they're like all the people we knew before the exodus; they were born with that memory embedded in their skulls, and don't give it any more thought than a stray lock of hair or a beauty spot.

We're the nth generation... It's been such a long time, but now and then, the most ordinary things stupefy me; how can I put it?... Sometimes my memory vanishes, and gives way to a kind of astonishment: for instance, I get up in the morning, look through the window at the sun, the trees, and the big meadow, and suddenly think, "It's really marvelous, but why are all these things there before my eyes? I'm seeing them for the first time, and don't even know their names." It's as if the world were beginning in that moment.

Mother sometimes says I get worked up over little things. Am I normal? Just because we're children doesn't mean we can always have fun, playing this or that to pass the time.

If you could speak from your beautiful future, no doubt you'd tell me what could happen to me. You'd talk to me about those fine tomorrows. They're fascinating to me. And you'd tell me who the puppet master is, holding the control bar. But in fact, aren't you the one pulling the strings? Please tell me honestly!

I'm not afraid of hearing anything you might have to say, and you've nothing to fear from me. Whoever you are, I'm begging you, answer me!

For that matter, if you truly exist, if you're able to hear me, maybe you could try to come? There's still room in the Borders. There's a bedroom in the loft that won't stay shut forever. Daddy says we could turn the living room into a bedroom, if we ever have to accommodate other refugees. Do we really need a living room? The kitchen is fairly large; we could gather there to read, draw, play, and chat in peace, as well as for our paltry meals. Do you want to play with us? Come closer, if you can.

✦

Nik and Rob have snuck away from the Borders. I hear them chatting as they go along, in the vicinity of La Croix Rampau. I press my fists against my temples, shut my eyes, and think, very hard, "Come back! Come back!"

Soon they'll be in the lower ruins of Poleymieux, and there, nothing can protect them anymore from the starving ferals, the giant rats, the Ashen, and the Scarraged.

Their words and thoughts grow faint; now I can only make out scattered phrases.

"You can tell me..."

"No, it's a secret."

"... Join the processions."

"... Too risky."

"No more electricity, soon no more water... wait for what?"

"... And if the Scarraged attack? You know very well what they did to me!"

"Scaredy-cat..."

"Cut it out, Nik!"

"Let's go explore over there..."

"Don't shout like that, or they'll…"

"My mind's made up, Rob, I'm leaving…"

I think, with all my strength, "Come back! Please…" No matter – they can't hear me. They're already among the ruins; it's too far away, I can't catch anything. Should I warn my parents? If I do, Mother will be sick with worry, and Daddy will want to catch them up; that will make three people in danger, instead of two… Oh, I'd just as soon know nothing about it, and never read other people's thoughts anymore!

I'm unhappy; I hide behind a bush, huddled up on the ground. I keep a lookout on the gate of the Borders, hoping my brothers will change their mind and come back the way they went… I shiver in spite of the overwhelming heat.

Ludo is running through the garden; he looks everywhere for me. I'd rather he didn't find me. I need to be alone; if he sees my head poking out from the bushes, he'll call our parents, and I'll be forced to explain everything. I make myself quite small. My ears are buzzing. Certain words rush into my mouth; I feel like crying out: *Lam… lim… lumi…*

Why would my parents be afraid of hearing a word? When they were children like us, didn't they like the story of *The Tower Carousel*, and the words of the *Song of the Free*? Are there parents somewhere in the world who remember what it was like to be children?

"Come back, you two! Come back, my darlings!" I shiver and sob. Perhaps we'll never see them again…

"Come here right now, Solène! Where are you hiding?" Mother and Ludo are looking for me; I squeeze up behind the bush and put a little pile of dead leaves on my yellow shoes, so that my feet can't be seen from the garden path.

"Come back! Come back!" Where are they by now? Among the white ashes? In the rubble? Among the brambles and nettles? Being pursued by giant rats? Getting attacked by the Scarraged?

Have they found other refugees? Families like ours, mutant vagabonds? Processions of children? Have they spoken to other children?

My nose is bleeding. All the questions mingle in my head and form a painful spiral. "Come back! Come back!" At my feet, red ants are gathering and preparing to climb up my legs.

I can make out my father, plunged in his fossil collections: he's enumerating, correcting, calculating. But rocks aren't going to get us out of this! He's double-checking, splitting hairs. "Ooliths..., let's label little a, little b, little c..." I've got no patience for this! How can anyone analyze a lot of ordinary rocks when my brothers are in danger? I feel guilty; should I tell him? Yes... no, I mustn't. But why haven't my parents called Rob and Nik yet since they left? Perhaps they simply think my brothers are messing around in their room.

"Come back! Come back!" What if they've found shelter elsewhere? What if they've found shelter in another house, another family? And if they stayed in that other house? If they forgot us forever?

Or else I think to myself that they'll have gone far away, that they'll have tried to join the processions. They'd be walking in the direction of the sea, only without us... "Come back! Come back, I'm begging you!"

The sun is setting slowly. The evening light becomes purple and brown. The wind picks up; swirls of dust dance in the air above the gravel paths; a piece of slate falls from the roof; a green magpie tries to fly against the wind. Mother hums the air from her cantata; in the living room, Ludo is learning a magic trick with colored balls, for he wants to impress us tonight; and as for me, I'm very unhappy; everything around me... red sun, dust, fossils, cantata, noisy magpie, silly magic – all this seems ridiculous to me, and doesn't bode well.

Suddenly I hear voices.

"That was a narrow escape!"

"Go on! They don't run as fast as us!"

"It's your fault, we almost got lost!"

"You think Mother and Daddy are worried? It's not that late."

Rob and Nik open the gate and run gleefully to the steps. Their clothes are torn, and I see that their hands and faces have been scratched by brambles, or animals; they're roaring with laughter, proud of their escapade. I leave my hiding place and call them.

Nik turns around. "So, you were spying on us as usual, Solène?" I shrug. "Swear you won't say anything!"

"I swear."

"And why are you crying?"

At supper, my mother is worried about the scratches she sees on my brothers' faces and hands. I come to their defense straightaway; I say they had a play fight behind the garden pond. "Oh! I thought you were in your room," my father says. He's not really listening; he's lost in his learned thoughts. "Let's label A, B, C, then A_{n-x}, B_{n-y}, C_{n-z}..." I'm dying to question my brothers: how did they outwit the Scarraged and the Ashen? Did they meet refugees, or children like us?

I carefully observe Rob's neck, then Nik's. I notice grey patches, like archipelagos on a map of the world. They aren't nettle stings. My heart beats very fast. Did it happen on the way back? At the close of the day? In the shadow of the setting sun's rays, before they made it to the protected zone? In that case, they can scrub and wash all they want – it won't ever go away. The marks of the lethal shadows don't fade. They stay that way, or else they spread bit by bit across the entire body. Have my father and mother seen these grey patches? Are they purposely keeping silent? Have they already forgotten everything?

✦

The air is cold. The wind blows in gusts. There are no clouds, but at the close of day, the sky is covered at once with brown patches that form and break up again, shimmering gently. Some patches turn to red, others to clear yellow. They swell and contract, gather together and disperse in the air.

The sky at the moment is covered with black commas, moving about in all directions. My father already saw them yesterday; casually, he said, "They're nothing but fossil thoughts," then went to his study without a second glance at the marvelous sight.

Now the black commas gather in hundreds. My father was wrong – they're not fossil thoughts, but birds, diamond kheras, simple passerines from the lakes of Africa, whose migration has begun. That means these well-known birds have succeeded in crossing the seas without being exterminated by the shadows; it's something to bring joy to refugee families, if our customs haven't disappeared, for kheras are the birds that watch over the birth of children and pets.

The kheras pour forth from the southern horizon, quite high in the sky. They seem disoriented at first, but gather fairly quickly to the west in long wheeling lines; then they cut back toward the east at headlong speed. I love the figures they trace as they soar through the sky.

The black birds come together and scatter in the blink of an eye! Not a cry, not a song; not even a chirrup. For that matter, the other birds have gone quiet, as well as the ferals, the hyenas and the carnobas. Silence reigns. My passerines slip through the air. At this point, they occupy the entire visible surface of the sky, calmly, without jostling, even though they keep changing places each instant.

Some of them rise and trace majestic curves; others drop in a dive and climb again gracefully. I never see them beat their wings; they let themselves be carried by the whirlwinds of air that seem to guide them.

Now and then, groups form, turn in a circle, hang suspended, and disperse all of a sudden, as if they were obeying some invisible signal. I wish I were able to attract their attention! I'm drunk with joy: *Lim... lam... lumi...* If I weren't afraid that my parents and brothers would hear me, I would shout this word that's been burning my throat for ages... Perhaps the kheras want me to cry out, or to sing them a song? They're flying in silence...

I hope to draw them toward us, to touch them, just for an instant! Are they aggressive or affectionate? Likeable? Gentle? These passerines are graceful, without question, but as for being gentle... I'm not so sure. Apparently they tear their enemies' faces with their little talons, and gouge their eyes out with their beaks. I love them just the same – it's in my nature. They must feel that, right? So I fix my gaze on them and wait: I don't want night to fall before they approach the Borders.

Here are the first birds, arriving as scouts; they pass above my copper beech, above the big meadow and the clumps of trees. I count six of them. They're blue and black, speckled with silvery grey. I'm sending them to you. Oh, please don't chase them away, it would bring you misfortune!

Six birds at nighttime
flying pirouettes
the first goes mad
and gobbles up his nest

Five birds at nighttime
blindly flying quick
the second goes mad
and gobbles up her chick

Four birds at nighttime
somersaulting round
the third goes mad
and the fourth can't be found

The night is very ill
four three two one nil
if you don't chase the birds away
death surely will

✦

Since everyone in the Borders is asleep, I'm going to tell myself
a story for someone my age, and even if no one in the world ever
hears it, I want this story to be embedded in me just the same!

This happened either before or after the time of the mangle-
words and the lethal shadows – it depends where you are.

Once upon a time, there was an old woman who lived in
Poleymieux, not far from Lyon, in a vast residence with closed
shutters. Over the years, her father and mother, her sisters and
brothers, her husband and children – all her family had left
her... such that she now found herself alone, utterly alone. She
grew so pale and feeble that a violent gust of wind could have
finished her off. She lived hidden away in a single room amid
mounting disorder. Every night, she opened the curtains, the
windows on either side, and the shutter in her room, in order
to observe a clump of flowers, bushes, trees, and a great copper
beech at the bottom of the garden, as well as a few somber ruins,
the grey sky, and the mountains toward the horizon in the east.
And there, when the sorrow of past partings drove her to the
darkness in her room, she struggled for air, brought her hands
up to her throat, and thought she would soon die. But at that
very instant, she awoke in her bed with a book in her hands, in

the prime of life, her finger resting on the following phrase of a tale she had read before succumbing to sleep: ... *become so pale and feeble that a nasty gust of wind could have finished her off...*, and her eye fell on the motionless phrase, which now brought her an intense and wild joy.

And here is a twin tale to help you, whoever you are – prince or princess of the night – to find sleep and peace.

Once upon a time, there was a girl in the prime of life who lived in Poleymieux, not far from Lyon, in a vast residence with closed shutters. Over the years, her father and mother, her sisters and brothers – all her family had left her... such that she now found herself alone, utterly alone. She grew so pale and feeble that a violent gust of wind could have finished her off. She lived in a single room, and alerted no one to her presence. Every morning, she opened the curtains, the windows on either side, and the shutter in her room, in order to observe, in the brightness at the bottom of the garden, a clump of flowers, bushes, trees, a majestic copper beech, the blue sky, and the mauve cut-outs of mountains toward the horizon in the east. She smiled at this new world. But at that very instant, she awoke in her bed, worn out by the years, with a book in her hands, and a trembling finger resting on the following phrase of a tale she had strained to read before succumbing to sleep: ... *the blue sky, the mauve cut-outs of mountains...*, and her eye fell on this blinding phrase, which caused her infinite grief.

How is it possible? Day is already here, and I didn't close my eyes once during the night! I can hear people busying themselves in the kitchen below. Mother's calling me. "Solène, you've been in bed long enough! Time to get up, the tea's ready!"

✦

Nik gets up, his hair a mess, his eyes shining with excitement.

He hums six notes, high and low, but since his voice is breaking, the melody is indistinct. He dresses quickly and comes down to the kitchen. He's the last one this morning. Mother has left him a bowl of tea and two dry biscuits. He enters the kitchen and hastily consumes his breakfast, while our mother dries the dishes from the last meal and puts them away. She pretends not to notice her son's presence, but I know very well she's thinking of nothing but him, for she fears the words he'll soon utter.

He goes up to her, takes her in his arms, and asks her to sit down. I imagine he's stroking Mother's cheeks with the back of his hand, as he does whenever he wants to be forgiven for something.

Even though my thoughts at this moment are trained on my mother and Nik, I'm at the bottom of the garden with my father, in the vegetable patch we began cultivating shortly after we arrived at the Borders. My father prods me, saying, "What are you daydreaming about? It doesn't take an hour to pull up a few yams!" I reply that he knows perfectly well what (and whom) I'm thinking about at this moment. He turns pale, his jaw drops, and he points at me, shaking his head, then turns his back, muttering, "What a nerve! What a nerve!" Bending over two tomato plants that are in need of watering, he adds, "Why can't you leave your mother in peace?"

In the living room, Nik has sat down beside the game of patience, and is reflecting quietly. He can't manage to say to Mother, "I'd like to go away, I'd like to try my luck elsewhere..." Mother watches him surreptitiously, and thinks that time should stop and then go back to before the exodus. She sees Nik when he was small; she sees the beautiful apartment in Lyon-la-Neuve. She touches my brother's shoulder. He gets up; she clings to him, and tugs on his clothes as if he were now at risk of flying away. Nik thinks, "I'd like to go," and shuts his eyes so as not to meet his mother's gaze. He fears she'll allude to his early childhood, to happy times gone by; if she does, he'll get up and leave the room without a word, to avoid bursting into tears.

I'm dying to cry out to Nik, "Whatever you do, don't go! You've already been hurt by the shadows! Stay with us. We have to come through it *the high way!*" I couldn't say how or why such a phrase came into my head, just after the word *lam... lim... lumi...*, which is forcing its way into my throat. If Nik could hear my thoughts as you can at this moment, would he listen to me? I know very well what I'm talking about! All that growling at night, over there at the edge of the protected zone, in the ruins of Poleymieux, in the fallow lands... all that lamentable wailing, those groans, those movements... I hear them more and more, day after day, at certain hours of the evening; I know that if one of us strays beyond the protected zone, they'll be destroyed, either by those creatures or the lethal shadows.

Finally, Nik looks Mother in the eye, and falters in a low voice, "I'd like to leave... to try my luck, you understand?" Mother says yes and no; she understands, and yet doesn't understand; all of a sudden, she rubs her son's neck with a towel, and asks, "What have you got there? Those grey patches... wash them off, or if it's an allergy, ask your father for ointment."

"It's nothing – really. Let me leave."

Mother wavers; chaos is everywhere – in her heart, in her head, outside, inside, yesterday, tomorrow. She no longer recognizes the marks of the scourge. I suffer with her; I hear her grief. I suffer with my brother as he kisses my mother's hair while she lowers herself onto a chair, her head in her hands.

A terrible thought frightens me: what if forgetfulness is devouring our memories and thoughts, just like the dirty shadows devour our bodies?

"Careful, Solène, watch what you're doing! You nearly hit me with your spade!" I murmur an excuse, and lower my head so as to see nothing but the brown, dry ground. Soon, Daddy and

I return from the garden with a few vegetables. Mother looks at us dumbfounded, as if we were two apparitions. My father announces in a playful voice that he's going to fix us an excellent meal with the fruits of our harvest and a few slices of dried meat.

We're soon having lunch in the garden. The rays of the midday sun caress our faces. Rob is in a good mood, telling stories. I don't say a word, not even so much as a yes or a no.

We're all hungry, but don't say so. I'm getting thinner, but Rob and Ludo are putting on weight; how do they do it? I don't know. Ludo abruptly wants to play see-through-hands with me, or mummies, or morra. No thank you. Besides, I don't feel well. My sight is blurry, and the voices of my parents and brothers blend together. A nasty migraine squeezes my temples with crab pincers. My thoughts are a stew of rotten fruit, and if I try to talk, my tongue feels all coated. I need to be alone. I must have complete calm.

I hide away in the lean-to, behind the firewood, underneath the sackcloth. My nose is bleeding – drat! My dress is stained with blood, but I won't budge from here until the evening meal. I think of bees, the smell of ants, a six-note song running through my head, processions of children, ocean waves and passerines.

Over the course of the afternoon, my brothers call me, and then go scouring through all the rooms of the house. They won't come into the lean-to, since my thoughts put up a barrier as soon as they get near. They're presently a few feet from this place, and Rob keeps saying the same thing: "So where have we got to?" Then they go away again in the opposite direction. Nik organizes a beat, all the way to the bottom of the garden and around the pond, as if I were nothing but a wild coypu!

It's strange that my parents are losing interest in my absence... That hurts, because after all, I could just as well have wanted to leave the Borders too, to go wandering toward the ruins and the fallow lands; I could run a great risk, like Rob and Nik not all that long ago... But that's precisely what they don't know, or what they didn't want to know.

"What if she's been taken? What if she ran away? What if the Scarraged bit her? What if she got hurt by the shadows?" Ludo keeps on questioning his brothers, who tease him. He insists. "Well, if a Scarraged one attacked *me*, I'd kill it with this!" I imagine that *this* is a small branch out of which Ludo has made himself a sling. I chuckle in my corner, but not too loudly, so that they don't hear me. At last they go away and get tired of looking. According to Nik, "Solène is showing off as usual. She'll reappear in her own time, when she feels like it..."

Later, in the living room, my father tells Mother that the stray cats have returned, that he saw at least six creeping around the garden before dawn, that the pitiful creatures are dying of hunger, and that they would be quite capable of ganging up to attack a child. He adds, "I'm afraid the protected zone won't be protected much longer. I detected a few weak spots in the barrier."

The sun going down sets fire to the horizon, and wounds the clouds that linger on all sides. Long diagonal rays play with the tree branches, stretch across the garden, and penetrate the living room, where I'm nowhere to be seen. My parents finally become concerned about my absence, and say they'll only have supper once I've been found. Time goes by; it's getting dark. Rob is increasingly annoyed. "Come on, let's eat without her! I'm so hungry!"

When night has fallen, I come out of my hiding place and walk through the garden. Personally, I'm not hungry. I want to play ball against the side of the house. My father approaches, his hand like a visor over his eyes, trying to pierce the night. Twice, he asks, "Are you there?" He advances toward me, one arm extended in front of him. I turn toward him, looking elsewhere, while my right hand continues to bounce the ball against the wall – the red ball he gave me for my birthday.

In the darkness, my father sees the whites of my eyes gleaming; he perceives the spots of blood on my lips and neck; he sees the red streak of the ball striking the wall with a dull thud. He opens his mouth wide to say something, then decides against it.

✦

"Listen carefully, Ludo! All six of us were in the mountains, and…"

"No, stop, Solène, I already know you're going to tell me a nightmare. You're scaring me on purpose! Let me sleep!"

"It's not what you think; I had a beautiful dream last night…"

Ludo puts his fingers in his ears, turns his head to the wall at his bedside, and shuts his eyes. "You can talk all you want, I can't hear you!"

"Too bad, I'll talk by myself, since you don't love me anymore… Long ago, before the exodus, you were very small; Mother had to carry you in her arms when we went out walking. We had an apartment in Lyon-la-Neuve, with lots of light and big windows. Our parents often used to laugh; you would run from one room to another; we were able to invent games; the entire street used to sing during the votive festival; we would eat stuffed fruit after hunting days, there were competitions for pastries, for kissing, for red magic, with prizes given out; there were candied fruits, cinephantoms, number games, even gliders above the roofs and the glasshouse windows; there were…"

Ludo unplugs his ears. He hops onto the floor and hurries over to me. We find ourselves face to face, sitting cross-legged on my unmade bed. He puts a finger to my lips, and says, "Solène, don't tell lies. You know perfectly well we weren't born before the exodus. It'd be better if you told me your real dream, the one you say you had last night…"

"Don't talk so loud, Ludo, they'll hear us."

"Is it a secret?"

"Yes, a big secret. It goes like this..."

All six of us are in the mountains, and walking slowly because of the scree. At present we're following a narrow path among blocks of stone and jagged rocks. It goes on so long that we're exhausted.

We come to the edge of a black lake that shines like a mirror. We have to climb into a long small boat. It will soon be night, but our bodies are glinting, along with everything in view. I'm seated across from you in the boat. You rub your eyes and yawn. It's not cold, and yet a whitish mist escapes from our mouths with each breath. The boat advances slowly through the water. A streak of passerines is flying behind the boat. They go at our pace, without beating their wings. The only sound we hear is that of the water lapping against the boat.

We've reached the far shore of the lake; the shore we set out from is no more than a grey ribbon in the distance. We land on a beach of white sand. Before us is a forest of trees with what looks like birch bark, but instead of leaves, they have white flowers hanging down like strips of fabric. We go through the forest, skirting the lakeshore. There are no people, no houses, no ruins. I wonder what's become of the birds that were following us. Daddy says we have to walk further and further if we want to get to the end. I'm not at all sure, so in my head, silently, I call on Grandpa Welldigger – you know, the collector of children's voices... You've often been told about him; he died just before you were born.

"I don't believe that, Solène! Dead people don't come back. Their words do, maybe, but not them! I'm telling you, I don't like this story one bit."

"You're wrong, Ludo, the elders talk to us in our dreams. As I was saying..."

Grandpa Welldigger answers, "I'm on my way," but since

I don't see anyone, I call on him again, and suddenly I see him coming up to meet us. Our parents are delighted. Daddy embraces him, saying: What a pleasant surprise! Welldigger looks at us all fondly, and begins counting, pointing at each of us in turn: 1, Daddy; 2, Mother; 3, Nik; 4, Rob; 5, Solène; 6, Ludo. Then he's amazed. "What have you done with the seventh?" Our parents lower their eyes and say nothing. Grandpa is angry, and says with a sigh, "He won't be long catching up to us. Solène, I'm counting on you!" Then Welldigger disappears somewhere into the white forest. We resume our trek. Nik shakes the branches, and the flowers fall like rain. We figure out that these worn-looking flowers are edible; it couldn't have come at a better time, since we're very hungry. The flowers taste of meringue and baoulé. They're really delicious.

Later, I turn around and see that the lake has changed. It's covered with fluorescent insects moving on the surface of the water. My throat hurts; a terrible word moves my tongue and forces itself to my lips: *Lam... lim... lumi...*

"Hush, Solène! Please!"

"Don't worry. I'm telling you, that's all..."

We come out of the forest; the lakeshore is receding. We cross a vast expanse of snow and snow dunes. Mother notices some snow huts; we go into one of them. It's really nice, believe me, because the snow is lukewarm. There's only one room in this hut. Everyone has their own snow armchair, and sits down gently. We eventually fall asleep, and all end up dreaming the same thing: that we live in a villa like the Borders, above the ruins of Lyon where the scourge has ravaged everything, but that we'll wake up thinking: it's all right, because it's a dream.

"Solène, stop pulling my leg! You say that Lyon and the Borders are a bad dream, but that the snow house, the edible flowers and the lukewarm snow exist for real. It's the other way round. I don't believe you."

"No, I'm not pulling your leg. I'm telling you exactly what happened; for that matter, since you were in this dream, I'm sure you'll remember it yourself – in a little while, maybe, when you go back to sleep. Now, listen, and don't interrupt..."

So, we'd fallen asleep in those snow armchairs. I'm the first to wake up, feeling refreshed. I leave the hut and see, right in the middle of the sky, a tiny blue dot in a constellation toward the south.

"What's a constellation?"

"A group of stars."

"Do stars really exist?"

"Yes, but not constellations. Those are drawings."

"But drawings exist too. I like to draw."

"Daddy will explain the difference to you between the stars and the drawings."

"No, you explain, now!"

"Shush! I'm telling my dream. There was this blue star; I looked at it without blinking, and the more I looked at it, the more my head spun, as if I'd danced for too long. There were six notes in my head, a melody of six notes sung by one voice or several."

"What's that star called?"

"Mintaka."

"I'm too sleepy now. Goodnight, Solène."

Ludo gives me a kiss and climbs back into bed. As for me, I'm not sleepy. I turn off the bedside light, but get up all the same, and bring my face up to the windowpane. I hear the rustling of wings and claws against the glass. I press my mouth to the pane, and murmur, "Do you want me to open the window? No, my little treasures, you won't be coming in." I look up at the sky. There's only a single star, bright blue, like a faraway signal.

✦

Black, grey, golden yellow... dotted with red and blue. It advances along the edge of the lawn, and I reach out my hand. The thing bolts away instantly. I block its way with my foot. It changes direction. A kind of living tube contracts between its two extremities, forms a small arch, and slackens in order to move forward: tchick, tchack! Like that, jerkily. Then it crawls on, undisturbed.

On its back I see yellow bands. The head is caramel brown. I don't much like this tiny shriveled face, which looks like it's ringed with black make-up. On either side of the head is a black wart with stiff bristles like cactus thorns. I have no wish to touch... Isn't it venomous? The body, for that matter, is covered with red and blue tubercles whose tufts of reddish-brown hairs are sticking out at me. Between the tubercles, the yellow skin appears smooth as rubber.

I take a stick and turn the thing over on its side, trying to wedge it against a small stone. It wriggles and curls up on itself, then plays dead.

My father is sketching in the garden; I know he's observing me from time to time, and won't be long in coming over. He'll look over my shoulder and admire my discovery.

Sure enough, here he is next to me, exclaiming with joy, "But that's Lymantria, the caterpillar of the bohemian moth! Magnificent! I'm glad you're setting out to learn things, rather than making mysteries and rummaging in other people's thoughts..."

"Does it sting?"

"Certainly it does, Solène! It has to protect itself before it can shed its skin and fly away. Let it go, and in a few days it will have become a moth."

"I don't think so."

"What do you mean, my dear?"

My father casts a suspicious look my way, and heads off to

the outer wall of the villa, in order to spy with a telescope on goodness knows what. Ludo joins me, sees the caterpillar, and takes a step back. "Oh!"

"Don't be frightened!" I tell him. "A container, quick. We're going to hide it by the hut." We put the creature in the carton that Ludo's found; I send my brother back to the house to fetch a pair of scissors; at that point we pierce small holes in the lid. The caterpillar has to breathe! We go over to the bottom of the garden, next to our hiding place among the box trees in front of the copper beech. Finally, we bury the carton between roots, and cover it with moss to conceal it.

In the evening, I settle in the living room and draw a few moths as I imagine them. I empty my mind. A song is resonating in me. I hum it, not knowing the words. It's a wordless melody, a refrain of six notes that says everything without words.

It's getting late. "Bedtime, children!" All of a sudden, the current begins to flicker, raising fears of a long outage. Two lighting tubes go out, after some crackling and a few bursts of sparks. Daddy replaces them, but it doesn't work. He speaks with Mother in a hushed voice; they seem worried. Personally, I'm not bothered, for I can see in the dark; I get that from my father... but he's very defensive about his night vision, as if it were a source of shame. I can make out what he's thinking: "It's an anomaly! I'm not a cat, after all!"

I have to think of the others first; I shouldn't like Ludo to be frightened in the dark. And I think of Mother most of all, so fragile. I approach her and look at her tenderly. "I can see your eyes, Mother dear."

Electricity is important. For us, water isn't as serious, even if it becomes earthy or dirty from the faucet. Several power cuts have been noticed recently, but we can cope, my father says. Indeed, we're lucky enough to have a pond at the bottom of the garden, between the tall trees and the new vegetable patch. I'm well aware the pond is brackish, but Nik claims that installing two filter nozzles would do the trick; he and Rob volunteer to fill goatskins with filtered water every day and carry them to the house. "They're tough boys," my mother says proudly.

Nik has been very attentive to Mother for the last several days. His thoughts are no longer directed toward the sea, the processions of children, exile, and all those perilous adventures. At this point, I don't think he'll leave us anymore, and I'm somewhat reassured.

Our supplies are running out. Daddy says we could easily kill and eat the ferals that have infiltrated our grounds ever since the protection became insufficient to keep them away, but personally I find that disgusting; I have no desire to eat cats, not even half-wild ones.

Another source of worry: I've seen grey patches on Daddy's left forearm. I also saw that Nik and Rob's grey patches hadn't gone away since their escape beyond Poleymieux. We should all know where we stand, and yet we don't speak about it! Why does everyone act like the patches had vanished? I shouldn't have kept the promise I made to Nik. I should have confided to my parents that he and Rob had been contaminated among the ruins.

But it gets worse: ever since my father noticed certain weak spots in the protection, ever since we started experiencing electrical outages, several carnivorous beasts have found their way into our domain. Could the Scarraged find their way in as well? I don't think so; they're ferocious, but too handicapped to withstand the shock, especially the oldest ones who've regressed into infancy, very weak, incapable of scaling a wall. Even so, my father claims to have seen certain Ashen trying to pass through the outer wall on the west side.

The Ashen live in hordes among the ruins, in the cellars, so their main enemies are the mutant rats. The Ashen have greyish-blue skin that looks like clay. People claim this skin protects them from the lethal shadows, but I really don't feel like trying to find out. It's said that their bodies, similar to ours, are feverish – warmer than ours, at least. It's said they bring up their newborns in chrysalises, which the mothers carry like sacks on their shoulders. It's said they have very sharp sight and hearing, and that they're agile like geckos; that they move around every which way, a lot faster than galabries, in order to throw off their foes. They sleep with their eyes wide open; they see at night, they're on the move at night. They eat mostly grass and roots, but also the dried meat of their enemies. Their eyes never blink.

One day, I came across an Ashen one at the southwest edge of the Borders, to the right of the pond. I sat down quietly on the ground to watch him. Trying to come towards me, he knocked his head against the wall, and rubbed his forehead before sitting down in turn; then he looked at me, swiveled abruptly, and bounded off.

As he was looking at me, I felt a strange zigzagging thought in my head, one like the buzzing of a cicada. So what did he want to tell me? I don't have the slightest idea.

It's said the Ashen reproduce quickly, but that they regularly fall prey to the Scarraged and to carnivorous beasts. In order to defend themselves against assailants, they set formidable traps at the cellar entrances. Away from the cellars, when night has fallen, they pick and gather plants, roots, and all kinds of wild fruit for provisions; their running skill and the sharpness of their senses protect them from flesh eaters, more or less. At least, that's what my father says, though he hesitates between two opinions: sometimes he says their species won't survive long, and sometimes he wonders whether they're not already highly adapted to a new kind of survival. For me, whether they're *adapted* or not means nothing, since we're all threatened by the shadow scourge.

These Ashen, with their skin like clay – do they bleed like us? Do they have nosebleeds, for example? When the rats attack them, do they bleed? Is their blood red like ours?

✦

I'm walking in the night. Everyone is asleep. It feels good out; it smells of honey and resin. The sky is covered with stars. Hundreds of fireflies are scattered throughout the garden meadow. Why are they gathered together like that? These past few days, a few of them could be seen by the pond or the vegetable patch, but tonight there are so many of them that a halo of light hovers above the grass.

The night is warm. A light wind caresses me. I move barefoot through the grass. I walk among the fireflies, taking care not to hurt them; gently, I put one foot in front of the other and spread my arms, as if I were having to balance on a tightrope.

I go slowly to the edge of the pond and sit on the grass, making sure not to crush the fireflies. I move four of them out of the way. I pick them up gingerly between finger and thumb. They crawl in the hollow of my hand. Their tiny bodies are cold. I place them delicately on a flat stone, fold my arms, and look at the sky.

Stars and fireflies form the same constellations, according to the same patterns. I wonder if in other gardens, among the fallow lands of the Monts d'Or, fireflies are arranging themselves the same way.

Orion's constellation has left the south; it sits enthroned in the very center of the celestial vault. In the center of this constellation, Mintaka's blue star is shining. A song of six notes is running through my head. My heart beats quickly. The smell of honey and resin is intoxicating; I'm happy, but a bit wary too... on the lookout.

All of a sudden, I hear a humming getting nearer. A cloud of bees envelops me, brushes me, and turns endlessly around my body. I'm not afraid; no point in closing my eyes and mouth, they won't sting me. In my thoughts I tell them all is well; I ask them why they're dancing around me. By way of a reply, I feel a tickling in my mouth. An unfamiliar force thrusts my tongue against my teeth, parts my lips and forces me to pronounce: *Lam... lim... lumi...* I start to shiver, because... because I'm wondering... the time hasn't come for... hasn't come for... hasn't come for... hasn't come for... hasn't come for... hasn't come for... comefo cff... cff... hsmcf... aocmsff... cff... cff...

✦

Ludo's scratched his hand on a bramble bush. "See what happens when you go mushroom hunting!" I help him pick three shiny red hydnums; they're magnificent, but that doesn't console him. "Magnificent? I don't care! Can't you see I'm bleeding?" I lick the drops of blood on his injured hand. "There, you're all better." Then I lick his tears.

"Stop, Solène, don't do that!"

"Would you rather I sang you a song?" He sulks and doesn't answer.

Run along run along in the ruins of Lyon
can you see can you see that sated cat
bring seven boas into the world
the boas grow big
each one swallows seven doe rats
who were carrying seven kitten rats:
how many cats and boas and rats
in the city of Lyon?

"Shush, Solène! Your song isn't nice, and I hate counting!"

"Come on, it's easy! It's $1 + 7 + 49 + 2{,}401$, which makes 2,458. And all because of a mean old tomcat-boa! What a re-population! And that's just the start!"

"No, you're wrong, Solène; Daddy told me that all the animals, even the mutants, will be wiped out by the shadows, since they don't have protections."

"Well, aren't you a know-it-all!"

"So long, Solène – I'm going to go play see-through-hands with Mother."

I pick a bouquet of yellow fuselias and go off to the bottom of the garden to celebrate my beech tree. I put the bouquet in my shirt, and climb the tree with the help of the six wooden steps that Rob attached to the trunk. I perch in the hollow of the second fork; I attach my bouquet with red wool to the end of a branch pointing toward the south.

All the nearby bees have spotted my presence. They come to buzz around the tree. My heart is filled with a desire to... I don't know how to put it, a gentle desire... What I feel is so strong, I can hardly breathe.

But I look at the ruins of Lyon in the distance, and see the latest damage caused by the lethal shadows; I hear the cries and groans of many living beings, animal or human; soon they're going to disappear, and that makes me sad; the colorlessness continues to spread; everything is threatened. Do the bees understand these words, these thoughts, *sad... threatened...*? They circle around me relentlessly; I don't know how to explain to them, I feel lost...

Suddenly, a cracking sound beyond the trees and the wall of the Borders! A group of lemures has crashed against the barrier wall, but I can see clearly that one of them has succeeded in entering our zone through an invisible gap.

If our protection weakens, we'll soon be faced with an invasion of creatures, and will end up dying even before the lethal shadows have enveloped us.

If we get the better of the flesh eaters, a ring of bees still won't protect our family once it becomes necessary to establish a curfew and close the shutters late in the afternoon, as soon as the sun touches the peaks of the Monts d'Or, over behind the Borders, above the ruins of Poleymieux.

The wind is stirring the leaves of my beech tree. I stroke the silvery bark, as smooth as skin. I climb down from the tree slowly, so as not to risk falling headfirst.

✦

A fine rain burnishes the leaves and grass. The sky is clear. In the wide path behind the magnolia tree, Ludo, hidden under an umbrella too big for him, is inspecting the ground. He's decided to find treasure. What treasure, exactly? He has no idea, but he's looking.

Halfway down the slope, against the outer wall, he comes upon a dead cat, disemboweled, no doubt, by another animal: one of those mutant ferals that we've heard mewing every night for an eternity. Beside the remains, the hairs of which stick together with the rain, there's a gigantic anthill. Neither the cat nor the anthill were there the other day, I'd bet my neck on it!

The red ants are working busily by the hundreds in their monument of sand. The rain doesn't bother them – on the contrary! They're reinforcing the sides of their hill. I can clearly see the little round holes through which, from the base to the summit, their lines march quickly in and out, without ever running into one another. From these orifices of sand and mud, tunnels go deep into the darkness of the rooms, corridors, or hollows whose shape I can make out, as if my thoughts could follow them, clinging to the insects' quivering antennae.

Here, two columns come and go between the anthill and the cat's stomach. The little mandibles tear off tiny mouthfuls of raw cat, not to eat them right away, but to transport them to the heart of the city, just as we do with the dried meat of the coypus from which we can still make delicious meals. They're provisions.

Have the ants themselves been stricken by the shadows' carnage? How have they survived? Did they transform themselves? I don't have any idea. Ludo asks me how long it will take this insect army to finish off the carcass. I'm not sure. For that matter, the ants aren't alone; I notice white larvae swarming in the cat's wounds, while small worms, grey and transparent, attack the head, starting with the injured eye.

The anthill is there, rising up between a stone, the dead cat, and the roots of an old ash tree. Ludo bends down, his nostrils quivering; the smell of the ants is strong, like warm vinegar or sweat. We observe the dark red of their cuirasses, their heads armed with fine shears. Some of them are bearing loads – grains, pods, twigs, leaf ends – much bigger than their bodies; others carry only pieces of flesh and coagulated blood. And I see others that aren't carrying anything! Those ones circulate from one ant to another, stopping and starting, bolting suddenly; they go to the newcomers and give instructions; there's a mysterious traffic going on; inaudible messages are passed between antennae. This pleases me no end, and the more I'm drawn to the ants, the more I like this pungent, delicious smell wafting up toward my face.

Some ants are climbing, while others descend; their files meet, swerve away, and run side by side without ever bumping into each other. Here's one marking a pause, rubbing antennae with a passer-by to exchange urgent messages. Sometimes, one of them slips on a grain of sand, slides, rolls over, lands on its feet, and obstinately returns to its work.

This one here has just switched routes. Did it forget something at the bottom of the pyramid? Two others are pondering off to the side of the traffic. Lower down, a group of worker ants hollows out a new tunnel in the mound.

Ludo can't resist the temptation to disrupt this little world; he wedges a stick in the sandcastle, and the hustle and bustle immediately intensifies. What a crush! The lines go crazy; an army of butcher ants streams out of the wounds, returning hurriedly to the castle in ruins. Ludo smiles, but I'm angry. He's taken aback.

"Ludo, imagine if a giant did the same thing to the Borders!"

"No, it's completely different!"

I leave him in the middle of his mini-disaster, and go back to the house.

From the living room, I continue to watch my brother with my sharp owl eyes, and listen in to his cruel thoughts. The mist from my mouth against the windowpane blurs the view slightly. I wipe the condensation away and blow, and my breath comes back to me with a chocolaty smell. That's strange, for we haven't eaten anything like that for ages! I'm so hungry I could faint.

I'd like to eat a splendid cake, fruits, candied larvae, and plenty of other mouthwatering dishes I can't even conceive. Don't let go of the words that I'm giving you like so many foods. Don't let go of *ants, bees, thoughts, Ludo, Solène...*

I have only to imagine you in order to feel lost in a giant void. I have a feeling that one day soon, I'm going to fall silent for a long time, so I beg you, try to come toward me... And for my part, I'm going to try hurling a few words into the vast black emptiness separating us; perhaps these words will ricochet toward someone. Then, patiently, I'll try to hear you, and even touch you...

There, I'm beside you; I can make out a table, a bed, a lamp, your hands, your lips. Can you feel my hair against your cheek? You look up; you've just heard a noise approaching. You sniff the air around you. A smell of chocolate? Vervain? Red ants?

Honey? Moist earth? You dry your left hand with your right; whose tear is it? Mine? No, I don't believe you.

You know my name, you can clearly hear the questions racing through my head: what happened after the lethal shadows, after the mangle-words, after the decline of the Scarraged and the Ashen, after the ruins and dust, after the bursting of the protective bubbles, after the mutants of mutants of mutants, after the ferals, after the giant rats, after the delirious swarms of bees, after the firefly rituals, after the famines, after the processions? What happened between our exodus and your great freedom, your marvelous survival? If you can hear me, it's because you already know.

I have a feeling you can help me. Please, turn your face toward me. Take all the words I offer you, and lend me your own; let's synchronize our antennae and travel together though the tunnels of time. Touch my forehead; I can see your eyes.

If you'd prefer, I can teach you a song, the *Song of the Living*: the one that my parents' parents' parents were singing already, two stanzas lost in the depths of time, according to an ancient fable:

Slowly now, slowly now
Child here below
Slowly now, slowly now
Deathward you go

Come to me, come to me
Child in your bed
Come to me, come to me
Child of the dead

Ludo has completely destroyed the anthill. He stands up, breathes in deeply, and looks on his work with satisfaction.

Then he goes off to find some flat stones, lines them up on the carcass, and covers them with leaves. Only the smiling head of Mr. Cat peeks out a bit. A couple of blue magpies chatter, as if to announce the end of the ceremony.

A timid sun dries the drops of rain. The air smells of chocolate, vervain, honey, and moist earth. A cloud of mist lingers above the bushes and trees; it crowns the top of my beech.

◆

Nik isn't sleeping tonight. He's decided to repair his mirometer! As if all those lovely machines hadn't given up the ghost since the exodus! Bent over his machine, tapping with his fingertips, he makes the grey, yellow, and red dots flicker as they swarm like bees and ants on the screen.

Suddenly he stands up, raises his arms, says "Yes!" in a low voice, yawns, stretches, and goes back to bed. Before long, he gets up again, rummages through some objects piled up in a toy chest, pulls out a small glass piano, and plays six notes that the screen repeats in an echo. He does it a second time, and the screen replies. The music I can barely hear, but Nik's joy and feverish thoughts resonate in my head, stronger than the music.

I get up and press my ear to the dividing wall. The six notes reach me clearly; I recognize the melody, and shiver. I can hear Rob ask his brother, "Where's that music from? It's so beautiful..." My heart beats faster; I wake Ludo gently.

"Come here, Ludo, you have to hear this!"

"What is it, Solène? Your dream about the lake and the snow again?"

"No, it's the music... Come and listen in the big boys' room – it's very mysterious!"

Here we are, gathered around the mirometer. The screen diffuses a pale light, from which there emerges a blurred mask that moves. It looks like a baby pulling faces. Rob points to the image.

"Who's that? What is that thing? A face?"

Nik scratches his forehead. "No, not a face, unless... Look, there are hollows and bumps, like dimples, a chin, a nose... but no mouth, no ears and no eyes! I've never seen anything like it!"

Ludo puts his hand up. "I know! A baby who isn't born yet!"

"Of course not! You're really too little," Rob replies. "Embryos are in their mothers' tummy, not in mirometers!"

"Ah, that depends," says Ludo. "You can make them in a transparent bubble and then give them to a mother."

"Brilliant, pipsqueak. But look – this is a mirometer, not a reproductive globe. Open your eyes!"

I ask them to keep their voices down so as not to wake our parents. Ludo raises both hands to get our attention.

"We have to give it a name!"

"All right, little man," Rob replies, "but boy or girl? Is it *he, she, heshe*, is it an *it*, or nothing at all?"

In a low voice, I suggest, "It doesn't matter – I was thinking more like a little name lost in the air and looking for a place to land, *lam... lim... lumi...*"

Ludo clamps a hand over my mouth. "Shush, Solène! You know that hurts our parents! Think of Mother, why don't you!"

Nik teases us. "You won't convince me the house is haunted by a kind of secret baby... This whole thing is ridiculous!"

"But the six notes... the music behind that face, I know it," protests Ludo, "and you know it too, Solène! Tell them what it is!" Ludo's right, but I'm wary of talking about stars, Mintaka, and Grandpa Welldigger, for Nik and Rob would make fun of me. They couldn't understand.

Rob presses a button and the screen switches off. "I'm glad it's gone away," says Ludo. "It makes me really anxious." I put my hand on the back of his neck, and we return to our room. He's unable to go back to sleep, and harasses me with questions.

"Solène, do you think it's a ghost?"

"No no, of course not... You ought to know that ghosts, angels, apparitions... all of that hasn't existed for an eternity!"

"What's an eternity?"

"Let me sleep, you're annoying me."

"So, the face, is it a monster?"

"Leave me alone, you know perfectly well the monsters disappeared a long time ago, thanks to smart people like Daddy, for that matter!"

"Solène, maybe I'm too little, but tell me why that thing sings a baby song..."

"We'll think about it tomorrow. Go to sleep!"

"Okay, but tell me – do all babies have a father and a mother?"

"That depends... I'll explain tomorrow."

"No, now! Tell me now!"

"You know what I think, Ludo?"

"No, tell me!"

"I think it's time to question Mother and Daddy."

"What are you going to ask them?"

"The who, the what, the why. You don't find it strange that we're not allowed to go into the attic room?"

"You think Mother and Daddy are hiding something there, or someone?"

"You never know... It's time to ask them some questions before it's too late."

"Solène, you're scaring me with your mysteries."

"There, there, Ludo dear... Now – go to sleep!"

And while we're all sleeping peacefully, in Nik and Rob's

room the mirometer switches back on, all by itself. Flashes of heat illuminate our windows briefly. On the screen, a pink and grey face covered with pearly veins is moving; I can see it as though it were right there in front of me. I can hear the face humming six musical notes. Two yellow pupils shine in the dark.

✦

The same night, I sneak out of my room, go downstairs without making a noise, and head toward the garden; the gravel hurts my feet, but in a few strides I'm in the lukewarm grass; I lie on it and contemplate the dark blue sky. The color is so intense, it enfolds everything I see: house, copses, trees, flatlands, creatures roaming near the pond to quench their thirst.

Deep blue: these strange words come to me – from where?... I don't understand them. Have I forgotten my language? Who whispered these words to me? The sky is empty, without moon or stars, but the blue illumines everything.

Does the stars' disappearance change certain words? *Blue... stars*, I don't understand anymore; or else I hear these words empty of meaning, for it seems to me they've lost whatever meaning they could possibly have had before this blue night that enfolds everything in its color.

Deep blue: is it my mouth saying these words? Is it you? Is it your customs and beliefs? Your fears? I'm losing *blue*, I'm losing *stars* and *sky*; I'm afraid of losing everything if you don't help me.

Please – in my place, say *night sky*, *sky without stars*, and *deep blue*, then lift your head up in the night, like I'm doing now, and look at the sky: hasn't it always been so, ever since the beginning of time? Hasn't it always had this intense, calming color? But who was speaking of *stars*? Where are the patterns you call *stars*?

I see a sky *without stars*, and this color in which a person could sink and drown. Who is *Solène*? I think I'm soon going to forget. *Lam... lim... lumi...* Here, little one, come closer! Don't be frightened!

The words are going away, but peaceful thoughts coil up and unwind in me like silk ribbons: *Deep blue, deep blue*, and your voice, way out there, replies, and echoes back several words that look for somewhere to land:

> the blue deep and gentle
> blue gentle blue night
> deep night ever deeper
> blue night blue dark

Without stars? Truly? I know the word *without* when I'm hungry or thirsty. As a result of being *without* this or *without* that, Mother says we'll end up "passing away." Personally, I shouldn't like to die of hunger or thirst, or to be gnawed at by shadows. But who said we were going to die? I raise my arm and draw stars in the sky.

In the firmament I hang lanterns, pearls of red and yellow, letters of fire, balls, sparks, beams of light that shoot across the sky. Call them what you will: celestial bodies, wandering stars, constellations. I'm the one drawing them! You're the one who'll see them!

> *Abrekebri Brikabram Bracam*
> *Sam Sam Alouam Al Stam*
> *Zig Zag Zoug*
> Count to six
> And breathe in deep!

Well, there you go! That wasn't so bad... We're lying in the grass. The air is so soft! The smells of summer waft up from the ground, which the sun has warmed during the day. I could contemplate this unfamiliar blue for a lifetime.

My gaze travels across the sky like an arrow, carrying my body with it. I'm a fine blue dot flying towards Orion, according to my pattern of stars, an arrow pointing to the sapphire of Mintaka. I traverse the whole of this nighttime blue, further than all thoughts, and yet my body hasn't budged an inch!

The wind rustles the leaves; the branches of my beech tree sway back and forth, black against the dark blue. The trees are whispering. They're singing the color of this night without stars.

✦

Daddy and my older brothers are at the pond's edge. They check to see that the filter nozzles are working, refill the goatskins with drinkable water, and return with the load on their shoulders. They open the cellar door, go down the stone staircase, and gently set the skins on the cool paving stones.

We're in good shape for the next few days, then, for running water is being cut off more and more frequently. The taps are sputtering and coughing up a yellowish earthy liquid. Every evening, Mother fills up the sink, the washbasins, and the two bathtubs, in case the cuts leave us without water for our morning wash. Nik claims that the water tower on the hill is cracked, and that the lethal shadows have begun eating away at the cement and stone.

After water duty, Daddy and my brothers go to the vegetable patch; there isn't much to pick; everyone knows it takes more time to grow fruits and vegetables than it does to eat them. Fortunately, we have the glebas! They appeared not long after the spread of the shadows, on the rubble and ashes in the Rhône valley; they flourished under the bubbles where refugees like us live; my father says that the waves protecting us are "conducive to their proliferation." After every storm, runoff rainwater and seepage carry the spores into the earth, right up to our grounds, which makes it possible to pick them without taking the risk of wandering away from the Borders.

Glebas are pearly white mushrooms, round in shape, without feet or radicles; they can grow to the size of a child's head. Their flesh is pale and sticky, but firm; it's studded with grey venules, and smells like almonds and chestnuts. Based on our experience, glebas can be cut in fine slices and eaten raw with beechnut oil and lemon juice, or else grilled in coypu fat.

Mother has found a few jars of kevere in a cupboard! It's a spice that comes from lichen found on the balmy steppes of the pole, widely used before the exodus; when it's ground to a powder, you only need a pinch of it on food in order for incredibly varied smells to emerge: agar, cardamom, mace, galangal, Melegueta pepper, nutmeg, bloutia, nouioura, cantharides, cinnamon, tara, felfel, cloves, turmeric, ginger, iris, elbzar, lavender, rosebud, darelcini, lissan, belladonna, nigella, asnab, milkweed, cubeb, kheroua, ziggiberis... It can also smell of magnolia pollen, ground mayfly wings, formic acid, royal jelly, and coypu musk. Don't think I'm exaggerating; my father confirmed it all, from a to z.

Obviously, it's impossible to smell and appreciate all of these aromas at once! That's why we children were taught at a very young age to choose some spice or other "by autosuggestion" (my father's the one who says that), from the very first mouthful of a dish spiced with kevere. The child doesn't need to know all the names of the ingredients; he closes his eyes, concentrates on the particular spice his palate appreciates the most, and makes his choice, with a simple thought that says *yes* or *no* to a specific aroma. Then, everyone is accustomed to sharing with the others around the table the taste impressions they've gotten from the kevere; this family exchange can become quite animated.

Sometimes, the discussion of flavors can provoke a deafening uproar! Everyone wants to talk at once; people contradict each other and argue... Each person tries to think of the exact name of the aroma they've just smelled. Fortunately, my father is there to help us, for he's the specialist on plants and animals. In the discussions of kevere, I listen to what everyone says, and remain silent, for other words are burning my lips...

The day the jars of kevere are empty, we'll quickly grow tired of glebas. Mushrooms, morning, noon and night... The taste of chestnuts and moist earth will seem quite stale in the end...

Daddy and my brothers come back from the vegetable patch with a yam, a shriveled parsnip, and a cabbage; they say, "Not even a gleba today! It's hopeless!" It hasn't rained in a long time; the earth is dry. Our three gardeners look down in the mouth. I observe them keenly. On my brothers' necks and hands, the grey patches have spread; for the first time, I see patches on my father's left forearm. Why are they pretending not to notice them? I could speak to them and cry, "Grey patches!... Lethal shadows!... We're stricken!" But they wouldn't hear, they would hardly react, they would watch my lips move in astonishment...

The day is nearing an end, the sun is dropping toward the horizon; the sky is a dark red color. In the dangerous zones, it's the hour of the harmful shadows. Observing my father and brothers, I think to myself that the protection of the Borders has weakened further, and that invisible fissures are breaking up the barrier that should filter shadows and rays and block the invasion of mutant creatures.

Nik, Rob, and my father have stayed too long in the vegetable patch, looking for a few wild tubers to add to our meager sustenance. They'll have been exposed to the shadows of the low sun... In the coming days, the scourge will affect us all, even if we close the curtains and shutters, even if we decide to live in the darkness of the cellar.

I'm sitting beside Mother under the magnolia tree, biting my nails. "What is it, my darling? Are you worried about something?" My father passes by with his basket; he sees me crying silently. He assumes a detached air, and distances himself. To my mother, I reply, "It's nothing." I snuggle up to her, and think sadly, "We're all going to end up as shadows erased by shadows..." But another thought seizes me almost immediately: "Unless..." And for a long time, I repeat "unless... unless... unless...," like a poor refrain to a six-note tune.

✦

"Solène, are you asleep?"

"Hush, Ludo, I'm talking to the song."

"You mean to a singer?"

"No, it sings and I answer. It's like that."

"For real, or in a dream?"

"Look, it's the same thing! When you dream for real, everything happens in a dream..."

"Well, anyway, your dream woke me up; I heard you singing."

"You're the one who woke me up, more like!"

"Solène, I had a nightmare."

"Tell it to me, and it won't come back."

"I dreamed we were attacked by the shadows. I hid in a cupboard, but I was afraid of the dark and I had a nosebleed, like you when you think too hard... Do you think I'm going to get sick?"

"Absolutely not, Ludo. Go back to sleep, and let me find the song again."

"Solène, please, can I go in your dream?"

"Cut it out! Dreams are personal."

"Oh please, just for a bit!"

"Listen, Ludo, you can certainly have the same dream as me; your dream can coincide with mine, but it will be your dream and yours only – do you see what I mean?"

"No, you're a liar! I know perfectly well what you can do when you go into other people's thoughts! You can enter my dreams just fine, so take me into yours – please..."

"Bring you into my dream? I love you very much, but I don't know how to do that."

"Okay, well, can I go back to sleep and you come into my dream?"

"No thanks, I'd rather not have a bloody nose like you!"

"Solène, I'm serious, don't tease me!"

"Goodnight, little brother!"

"Solène, I'd like to talk to the song. Tell me how it's done..."

"Listen, here are six notes... you only have to learn them and repeat them in your head as you sleep."

Goodnight! Let's sleep tight. Go ahead without me, or else wait to hear the rest until I'm awake... or else...

Yes, come here, come into our room without making noise. The floor creaks, and the wardrobe moves imperceptibly. The darkness of the room is tinged with faint yellow glimmers that slip beneath the door and across the floor. Other glimmers come in through the shutter slits. Suddenly, the glimmers vanish. The blackness becomes so thick it could stifle you. Shush! There's the rustling of creatures... You say *insects*? A lot of them?

You're listening, you can no longer think, you can no longer move, you're perspiring freely, you're tormented by horrible itching sensations, you can't scratch. Impossible to call out, impossible to get away. You've become our guest. Your body slides along the slanting boards; the beds slide, scraping the floor. The partitions crack, and through the cracks comes a grey and pallid light. Far away, at the end of the sloping floorboards, you can see... a Solène in a white nightdress, undisturbed by anything: she opens her arms, lifts her eyes, hums... while the rug, the lamps, the chairs, the headboards and the beds move slowly before her without bumping into her. She's singing a six-note song. She's thinking of you, she's thinking that this little refrain has found a fertile soul in which to blossom... You've found me, at last.

✦

Late in the afternoon, my father says a storm is threatening. Sure enough, the cicadas have fallen silent, and the wind is banging the doors. We pick all the flowers the rain could damage. Nik has difficulty breathing; the anxiety and heat are tormenting him. He now knows the lethal shadows have wounded him; the grey patches go all the way up to his eye on his right cheek. He thinks to himself, "Things have gotten so bad that I have nothing more to lose, I would do just as well to try my luck elsewhere..."

"Try his luck elsewhere?" My poor thoughts can make out the cries of rage and panic, and the awful urges of the survivors confronting each other a mile or two from here. Any further than that, what I can see becomes blurry and gives me a migraine. But today, for the first time, around the Borders I can hear groans, mewing, squealing, a strange commotion that worries me.

In the ruins and the cellars, on the roads full of holes, rats, cats, hyenas, and hordes of Scarraged and Ashen are warring with each other. I can hear the moans of the refugees bitten by animals, the moans of other refugees bitten by refugees who are themselves contaminated by the animal bites, and so on... How to tell this to Nik, now, when he wants to "try his luck"?

Nik has me just about figured out; he takes the flowers I've picked, gives me a kiss, and says, "What does it matter what happens to me? In any case, one of these days, all those cruel gangs are going to run rampant."

"Please, change your words, it'll protect you!" I reply. And I add a phrase incomprehensible even to myself: "Yes – *let's change all the words!*" I don't know what came over me. The phrase surged up inside me, imperious, burning...

Nik looks at me, taken aback, and sighs with a shake of his head. "Poor little sister, you're so strange! We can't rely on you." I turn my back on him, hurt by his attitude, and go off to cut lavenders to complete the Agapanthus bouquets. Then I'll go play ball by myself, for I'd prefer to be left alone.

Daddy crosses the big meadow with an armful of flowers; he turns around and sees me playing against the door of the lean-to. I pretend not to see him, while with a deft hand I bounce the red ball, throw it, and catch it again numerous times without letting it drop. My father bends down and picks up a flower fallen on the gravel; he stands back up slowly and returns to the house without taking his eyes off me.

Above the Rhône valley, a heap of clouds is advancing; the summit is luminous and white, the base dark and flat. The mass progresses toward the northeast, becoming black and turbulent. We have to seek shelter. A strange fog slips beneath the clouds and clings to the treetops; the wind rages, hot and cold, swirling. Lightning cracks, thunder rolls, the torn clouds split off into several masses and break over the valley. A violent roar shakes the walls of the Borders. Thick rain beats down on the big meadow. Now, clusters of hailstones are striking walls and windows. A few spurts of hail come in through a window that hasn't been properly closed.

Very quickly, the sky clears again, like this morning; the mass of clouds has abruptly dissolved. The earth is steaming; broken branches line the ground, or hang partly broken off in the wind. The storm is over; patches of fog trail just above the ground like cloth.

Supper is gloomy in spite of the flowers adorning the table. Emergency biscuits, dried seaweed soup. Daddy murmurs, "Just as well, just as well; after a storm like that, we might find more glebas..."

I can't take my eyes off Nik's face, covered with grey blotches.

Mother watches him too, and says to herself, "It's best not to think about it." Her lips quiver. She closes her eyes and hums Montéclair's cantata.

✦

"Well, what did you see? Tell us!" Ludo grasps Nik's hands and looks at him intently. Nik and Rob have come into our room; they say their mirometer is no longer broken, that it began working again for a brief moment. They say they saw a façade on the screen, and a garden... a house identical to ours.

"Is that it? Just a view of the Borders?" Ludo is disappointed.

Nik grows impatient. "Listen! An image wobbled on the screen, and then we saw the outer wall of the villa, the gravel paths, the big meadow, and suddenly the entry gate opened all by itself... The view shifted from the gate to the front steps on the gravel. But as my eyes moved away from it, the image adjusted the viewpoint and the distance. That's how I managed to go in and out of the Borders several times, as though I were in a film on a loop, going from the steps to the entryway, the entryway to the hall, the hall to the living room, the living room to the hall, to the entryway, to the steps... and so on. By looking in a different direction, I could adjust the distance as I pleased; I was able to visit the entire house and garden, and look at the façades; but the house was empty, like it was abandoned... I tried to go through the gate and out on the path to Poleymieux, but then I saw another gravel path, another set of steps, another façade of the Borders; going to and from the Borders was becoming the same thing; every time I went out, I entered another domain of the Borders, doubled... tripled... the Borders infinitely multiplied; each time, the same house and garden – ours – as if the Borders were the only world there was, starting out at the Borders, ending up at the Borders, on all sides, endlessly. No place except the Borders and its big garden, from which we haven't dared venture since we've been staying here. I looked all around me, doubting the reality of our bedroom, and then at that precise instant, the screen crackled and the miromometer stopped working again. This time I think it's really done for."

"What about you, Rob? What did you see?" Ludo asks.

"The same thing. Everything he said is absolutely true."

After a long silence, I ask my brothers whether in all those views of the Borders they saw any inhabitants... children with their parents, for instance. Asking the question, I hide my worry; impossible to read my older brothers' thoughts. Nik scratches his chin; the grey patches have spread toward the top of his face and reached his forehead; tufts of hair are starting to fall out. Rob's right eye is greyish and swollen; he's constantly scratching his hands. I repeat my question, and after a moment's pause, Rob replies, "No, Solène, no one... no one and no sound."

Thinking of all those empty rooms, those floors, those hallways and bedrooms without a living soul makes my heart ache, and I cry silently. "But it's all right, Solène, they were only images. We're all here, don't worry!" As he says this, Rob scratches his neck violently. Grey scabs come away, to which he pays no attention. I reach toward his face, but he immediately turns away, murmuring, "No one and no sound..."

Nik, meanwhile, yawns and motions to us to leave. "There, you young ones know all there is to know. Goodnight now!"

Rob's last words return to echo in my head. "... no one and

no sound... no one, no sound..." Ludo is enchanted by the story of the repeating house, and he falls asleep laughing; as for me, I stay awake till dawn, repeating "no one and no sound." At last, when the haunting echo of this phrase ceases, the six-note song – the song of Mintaka – succeeds in calming me, and I fall asleep.

✦

It's happened late in the afternoon. I've asked my brothers to follow me to the bottom of the garden near the tall trees: here we are, all four of us, seated in a circle on wooden blocks in the hut.

"You're acting all mysterious," Nik says, to tease me.

"No, far from it – but I'm worried..."

"What is it you want to talk about?"

"I think we should take care of our parents."

"Oh really?" says Rob. "You don't think they're old enough to take care of themselves? It's not for us to protect them, after all!"

"Well, yes, in fact, it is," Nik responds. "Solène's right."

"What do we have to do?" Ludo asks nervously.

Nik answers. "We have to speak to them very soon, or else something bad's going to happen to us."

Ludo puts his arms around my neck and announces proudly, "My sister has a blue star; she knows a shiny lake and houses made of warm snow; she knows the song of Mintaka, she has..."

Rob cuts him off. "And I'm a great magician, I can change pebbles into pastries and ordinary sticks into coypu skewers! You're so gullible, little Ludo. You don't have to swallow everything she says!"

"Leave him alone, Rob," sighs Nik. "We really have to talk to our parents."

I choose this moment to utter a phrase that's been burning my lips since morning. "We have to ask them to go into the *white room* in the attic."

"How do you know it's white if we're not allowed to go there?"

"It's in Mother's thoughts. She often goes there in the morning before we're awake."

"Do you know what she does there?"

"I don't know, Nik. I can hear footsteps... she sorts through things. I can hear sighs, soft words, as if to lull a child to sleep."

"You think our parents are hiding someone in that room?"

"I don't have any idea. Perhaps it's their secret."

"What's the *white room*?" asks Ludo. Nobody answers. We return to the house.

Mother is waiting for us by the wisteria. "Where'd you go off to, my dears?"

"Nowhere, we were just having fun," I reply.

"Good, good..."

The sun is setting; a slanting ray of light shines on a corner of the big meadow, spreads across the gravel, and touches a patch of the façade. I go out of my way not to expose myself to the light or the shadows it casts; but I notice my father passing back and forth in the beam and the shadows, as if he'd forgotten that we're barely protected anymore. All of a sudden, the remark he made before the exodus comes back to me: "From the very first lesion, the people contaminated will forget what's happening to them." I shiver; my hands are freezing, and yet it's so warm out...

The cicadas are singing. Passerines, perched on the branches of the magnolia tree, are watching us with the closest attention. I suppose these pretty birds, returning from the devastated flatlands, will be gleaning their meager sustenance in the garden as soon as we've left.

✦

What will become of us? Tonight at the edge of the pond, I found the body of a Scarraged one covered in wounds, partially eaten by the ferals and rats. The intruder must have found a gap in the protection of the Borders zone; he'll have wanted to drink from the pond before dying. Ought we to bury these poor creatures?

In the same spot, I saw that the shadows had ruined the vegetation; nothing is left of the grass, the brooms, and the entire reed bed, save a grey dust and a few dry stems.

From now on, our parents are forbidding us to play further out than the big meadow. "I'm worried this rule won't be enough," my mother says, "for if the protection is weakening, before long the scourge will reach the house." My father shakes his head, but doesn't respond. Nik speculates. "If the vegetable patch and the pond are ruined, what are we going to eat and drink?" Once again, my father shakes his head without saying a word.

During the night, no one really sleeps. Everyone's anxious questions run through my head and make me nauseous. Suddenly I hear my father getting up. I think he's stumbling in his pajamas, which are too big for him. He goes into the hallway toward his study. He enters, sits in the old leather armchair, and has a long scratch of his hands and neck; he makes an effort to breath calmly.

Now I think he's getting up, lighting a torch lamp and casting the beam of light around the walls, the windows, and all the objects brought back from the laboratory in Lyon-la-Neuve at the time of the exodus. He examines his large table, bare and tidy, the bookshelves behind the table, the labels, and the numerical boxes that are no longer usable: *Genet. Res. Products. Gen. Gen. Know. Neonatal D. Gen & Her. Assortments.* He counts the boxes once, and then starts over.

Opposite the study door on either side of the windows are boards with moths, several species of *geometrida heterocena* –

those are my father's words. He talks to the Common Heath moth, the Scorched Carpet, the Small Emerald, the Double-striped Pug, as if the insects were still alive. Each moth is pinned and labeled, with its cocoon, caterpillar, and chrysalis. On the sidewalls are boards with bees, displayed with fragments of their hives. Lower down, in the gold frames, are photos of queen bees beside their brood.

On another wall he contemplates a few anatomical engravings, scratching his head: the human embryo at various stages of its development. The precision and delicacy of the drawings no longer move him. And yet the pastel blue of the veins... the bright red of the arteries... the pink, white and yellow of the flesh, depending on the organs... He touches his own face, and a question crosses his mind: "I should repair... I should... I should... but what exactly should I do?" Suddenly my father's thoughts freeze on the word *repair*; he repeats it several times, then... "What day is it? Since when?" He becomes dizzy, sits down heavily in the armchair, and counts on his fingers to ten, a hundred, a thousand... What good can it do to count like that? I want to go to him and console him. But why console him when he's not sad? I can feel clearly that he's not suffering.

Those wounded by the shadows no longer suffer – that's the way it is, up to the end. I think the shadows have damaged my father's thoughts, and it frightens me. He says *stones, calculi*. I remember what he told me when I was younger: calculi are stones produced by living organs, whether plant, animal, or human. In short, if I understand correctly, once in the ground we can all become stones... that is... more like dust at this point, since the shadows reduce everything to dust!

My father's head jerks back abruptly, and his eyes roll upwards; he begins stammering a whole series of stone-words, a strange collection of calculi he often dreamed of, before the exodus:

Bilirubin, bezoars or anti-venom stones, calculi of horses or talisman against snakebites, bezoars of deer, llamas, antelope, buffalo, and even owls and porcupines, canary yellow calculi of cat bladders, cerebellar whale calculus, gastric lithophysa of psychopathic stone swallowers, whelk valves, Shiva's eyes, baroque pearls (white, grey, black, pink) in crooked forms, children's milk teeth, ivory marbles, ossicles of fossil men, hyaline bones, coprolites, multicolored coral, Floridae of the atolls, reefs and other marine deposits; amber, succinite, dragon's blood, galipots, lignite, coal and diamonds of all kinds, nut stones, carapaces, nails and shells, fossils of all kinds, all fossils, the millions and millions of fossils, plant, animal, and human, the billions of animalcula, shelly limestone and calcified algae that have formed the sediments of the earth's crust; I want everything, everything, even the hopes and torments set by magic in limonite, moonstone, and partridge eyes; I want gallinacea, thunderstones, intaglios, abraxas and other false stones; I want jaspers, banded stones, orbicular ones, opalescent ones, landscaped ones; I want changing polychrome opals; those that glisten at night and those the voice can shatter; I want the imaginary stones, absolutely unalterable and unbreakable: angel tears, angel hairs and Lucifer claws, divine blood rubies, philosopher's spittle, drops of virgin milk, humors of incubus and succubus ghouls transformed into geodes of sulfur and arsenic; Titan teeth, Cerberus nails, Venusian menses flowed into cinnabar and mercury, crystals of morning dew, shards of rainbows and the aurora borealis, golem clay, hapax chaplets, Adamic and adamantine imprint of the first word spoken in the Great Mountain long ago! ... Ah... Aaah...!

My father has fainted. I leap out of bed and hurry to him. "Daddy dear, wake up, please! Oh, your poor head!" I kiss his forehead covered in sweat; I warm his grey and ice-cold hands. He sits up unsteadily, rises without looking at me, and staggers back to his room.

I pick up the torch lamp fallen on the rug, and shine the light on the binders, boxes, boards, and engravings, one by one; painstakingly I decipher the learned names that for me will only ever be combinations of noises and sounds, whose real meaning is hidden in the past of the old world. Where are the Wonders of the World, the ones Daddy used to tell me about at night before putting me to bed? All these fossils frighten me; I'd rather know the hummingbird of Tchimborae or the fire flower of Tchoukarawa... You think I'm rambling? So then, there aren't any Wonders of the World in your time?

Finally, I sit down at the large worktable. I open a drawer and take out a book with a brown leather cover; I open it with one hand, the other shining the torch on the pages. All of the pages are blank, except the first, which bears the enigmatic title: *Since the Dawn of Time*.

I flip through this empty book, and suddenly, right in the middle of one of the pages, I notice a tiny white form wriggling on the spotless paper. It's a small worm, whose waxy ringed body moves slowly across the page. It weaves its way between the white fibers, detaches one, two, three fibers with its very fine mandibles, and begins to hollow out a tunnel slantwise in the page, leaving a minuscule trace bit by bit, like a sort of writing whose barely visible form signifies nothing, not even for this creature who will be lifeless before long.

✦

Daylight is fading. Clouds of mayflies sweep down in front of the house on the gravel and the flower banks. A gust of wind tosses clusters of insects against the living room windows; their green-grey wings, crisscrossed by tiny pearly veins, cover the front steps.

These insects are nearly dead, yet the wind stirs them, and seems to give them added life before scattering them. My brothers gather them up by the handful. I run to join them, and do likewise; Mother comes out of the house, ordering us to throw the insects away and wash our hands afterward. "From now on, I forbid you to go out without wearing masks and gloves, not until the southerly winds have died down."

"It's pretty... it looks like sugar – I wonder if it's edible," thinks Ludo, for our supply of biscuits and dried seaweed has been exhausted for several days now. His question makes me think of yesterday evening; Nik and Rob were overexcited; they couldn't stop talking about fruit, vegetables, meat and fish, with which they were imagining fantastical recipes. By the end, everyone was arguing over the best recipe for coypu with oranges, and Ludo began to cry, wailing, "I want some! I want some!"

No childishness this evening... We absolutely have to avoid arguments and keep calm. Daddy is unwell. His voice is rising in pitch like a little boy's. My brothers and I are piling on the affectionate gestures to our parents. Ludo takes a mischievous pleasure in scampering from one to the other to whisper secrets. Mother bites her lip. She's constantly catching her breath, as if she were afraid of suffocating. She looks at each of us incessantly, one after the other. Is she afraid we'll disappear into the night, suddenly and without warning? My father assumes a knowing look, but doesn't listen to our conversations. His gaze wanders far off; his ailing thoughts stumble over words and numbers whose secret he's forgotten: "Tax... tax... taxon... Little a, little b, little c... tax... tax... taxon..." I stroke his right hand tenderly; the other hand, blotchy with grey, grinds a nutshell and picks up crumbs.

Nik leans over to me and whispers in my ear, "We decided! We have to talk to them tonight." I just nod my head in agreement. Mother thinks, "Oh, there's something brewing..." She gives Daddy a questioning look; she waits for him to take the initiative. He leans his head toward her, smiles, opens his

mouth, but remains lost in the detours of his thoughts: "Tax...
tax... taxonomy."

I'd very much like to assume a detached air, to look out the
window, for example... to examine the mayfly wings stuck to the
panes, but it seems to me that if I stop surreptitiously watching
my father, he'll end up completely immobilized like a statue.
Rob coughs and looks at Nik, as if to say, "Go on then! What are
you waiting for?"

Our frugal meal is over. Rob and Ludo are talking with Mother. She smiles and keeps saying, "Oh yes, my treasures!" Finally,
Nik, being the eldest, decides to speak for all four children. He
coughs several times, blushes, taps on the table with the handle
of his fork for Ludo and Rob to stop chatting, then takes the
plunge in a solemn voice. "Mother, Daddy, we've been thinking that... I mean, we've been discussing things, all four of us.
We've been thinking carefully..." – here he pauses for a deep
breath – "... we'd like to tell you that..."

Mother grasps Nik's arm, takes him by the shoulder, and
puts a hand over his mouth. "Hush, my child! I know what
you're going say... But what do you have against me? You're
going to bring on one of those... one of those..." But Rob gets up
immediately and says in a high-pitched voice, "Mother, please,
please... you mustn't get upset! We just want to talk to you." He
sits back down, overcome with emotion.

Ludo knocks over his chair as he gets up, and goes over to
huddle against his mother, bumping against the edge of the
table. He whispers in a small breathless voice, "Mother, Daddy,
please... Nik saw the face... the moving portrait, and Solène
heard the music, she says it's... that it's a... a thing that... Go on,
Nik, explain to Mother!"

My father gets up, closes his eyes to concentrate, and says
in a toneless voice, "I hear you perfectly well, children. Don't
think I haven't heard anything." Then he sits down and gives

me a wild look. Nik gets up again and declares loudly, "We have important things to say to you." This declaration prompts great confusion; Mother covers Ludo with kisses, humming to drown out our voices, and goes about clearing the table, clattering plates and dishes, while my father rises again and proclaims in a theatrical voice, "How can you...? To what end...? Given the situation, it's really not the moment to... At your age... How can you know whether..."

My mother's terror-stricken eyes look desperately for an object in the kitchen, something, anything to lean on, in order to avoid a conversation that hasn't even begun. She takes hold of both of Nik's hands; he hardly resists, avoiding her eyes above all, so as not to weaken. I stand up as straight as an *i*, my arms flat at my sides, and utter a shrill scream. Mother covers her ears; my father stammers, "But Solène, this is insane!" Nik then declares in an ill-assured voice, punctuating his words with quick movements of his right hand, "Mother, Daddy, it's your turn to speak... you've hidden him from us for too long. We want to go see him, all together, before..."

Nik lowers his head, stunned by his own audacity. I take over. "We'd like to go with you to the *white room*. Say yes, we'll follow you and behave, we won't say a word, we promise..."

Rob adds in a soothing voice, "Please say yes... We're not afraid... We could all give him a name together..."

My father jumps up and stands over Rob. "Who is this *he*? Forget it, my boy... Forget it, or you're asking for serious trouble. Leave us alone now. I'm... so tired." Then his thoughts return to a standstill over "tax... tax... taxon..."

Nik turns to Mother. "What should we be afraid of? We're here at home; everything that's happening is happening amongst us, in our house..."

Daddy interrupts him. "I'll tell you what there is to fear, you foolish boy! You're going to unleash a storm of mangle-words! You've been warned!"

I ask calmly, "Could we just go into the *white room*? We'll go in silently."

My father shrugs his shoulders. "Well, so be it... but at your own peril... You've asked for it! From now on, I take no responsibility." He sits down, mouth hanging open, arms dangling at his sides, worn out.

Nik fiddles nervously with a fork. Ludo complains he's still hungry. We're all numb, as if we'd just been walking for a long time into the wind. Silence reigns. I can hear a far-off siren, then mewing, the knock of a moth against the living room windowpane, and a few growls in the garden. All of these noises seem to say: Leave it... Let the night do its work, let it pass. Go to bed! And I hum six little notes, *fa do sol la mi la.*

Later in my bed, on the brink of sleep, I slip into the dreams of my brothers and my parents, then fall exquisitely into the void...

✦

The sun is getting ever lower. A terrible wind has risen. The shutters are banging. From the living room where I'm sitting, I can hear a moan and the sound of broken glass. The wind dies down for a moment, then comes back in gusts, howling, roaring against the doors, and slips into the house, deafening, full of crushed words.

I don't understand anything of these decayed languages, these mass murmurs; they're not real phrases, but coarse laughs mingled with groans, or else muffled blows endlessly repeated, moans followed by clapping, rhythmic steps, hoarse cries. The vibrations go through my flesh, vibrate in my stomach and skull. I hurt everywhere. I feel like throwing up.

The wind hurls bundles of words at us. They fall on us, buffeting us, battering us! Fragments of words crash repulsively to the ground, frayed, soaked in grey pulp... I don't dare move. I'm crouching in a corner of the living room, protecting my head with my hands. My brothers on the floor above are crying out with fear or anger; my parents are shouting orders incomprehensibly. I'm shivering with cold.

The storm lifts up whirlwinds of shredded words, throws them against the walls, catches them, and throws them again. All of these frantic phrases trail patches of shadow behind them, which try to cling on here and there. I shut my eyes so as not to see them slithering over the floor.

Wind and dust of mangle-words seep everywhere, even into the cracks in the walls and the floorboards. I crawl toward the staircase, and climb on my hands and knees as fast as I can without looking back. I see Ludo crouching on the landing. "Quick, quick! Look!" he says.

His arm is pointing toward the southwest skylight; the hallway rug is strewn with shards of glass. The orange rays of dusk color my brother's arms, face, and clothes. His hair is blown about by gusts of wind. He's very beautiful, but I'm terrified by the grey patch I can now see on the back of his neck.

We hear the roaring of words getting louder and louder. I hold Ludo very tightly in my arms. He covers his ears and moans, "No! Stop! Solène, tell them to stop!" But I'm powerless to do anything. Like him, I'm transfixed, lost. I'm no longer able to make out the thoughts of Nik and Rob or my parents. I think they're huddled in a corner like us, and that their cries or groans are drowned out by the howling of the wind.

The storm of mangle-words dominates everything, outside and in; it bypasses walls, shakes windows and doors, shatters panes, lifts the roof slates, breaks tree branches, pulls up flowers, and hurls itself against the façade of the Borders, trailing bundles of voracious shadows behind it.

I concentrate on a single word – Mintaka – and on the musical notes. I press my lips to Ludo's ear and sing *fa do sol la mi la, fa do sol la mi la*... without stopping, until I can no longer breathe.

Ludo and I are able to crawl to the door of our bedroom. In the hallway, the wind rushes in through the skylight, lifts the long garnet rug, and flings mangle-words against the partitions, where they break up, bounce off, and finally come crashing to the ground with a thud. Where have our parents gone? Where are Nik and Rob? Ludo calls to them, sobbing.

In our bedroom I seize my blue blanket. Ludo's teeth are chattering. He's sweating profusely; I dry him off hurriedly with old clothes and wrap him up in my blanket. "Be brave! Stay on the bed, Ludo, and don't move until I get back!"

"All right," he stammers, "but I'm shutting my eyes! Come back quickly, don't leave me all by myself!"

"Of course – I promise." I make my way with difficulty to the big boys' room, avoiding the pieces of glass that the wind has scattered over the hallway floor.

Nobody in Nik and Rob's room! I turn around and suddenly see Rob in his pajamas; he's coming out of the toilet, limping slightly. I repeat his name three times, cupping my hands to my mouth. He comes toward me, his hand over his mouth, as if he wanted to tell me to be quiet. He staggers and pitches forward onto his shadow. Right away he gets up, and examines his black hand with alarm. He turns away from me and struggles toward the bathroom. I call him again: "Rob, are you hurt? Answer me!" A blast of wind stops me going forward.

The sick light of dusk blinds me. Rob's shadow is embedded in the floor in front of the bathroom. I slip and fall on this black puddle, get up again, and look at my fingers, which have turned grey... I throw up on the floor, and think I'm going to faint; I fight to stay conscious.

I hear several muffled noises. They're coming from my father's study. I want to cross the hallway toward the study door, but twice the wind knocks me off my feet. I get back up and grip the door handle. The blasts of mangle-words rain down on me. My head hurts so much... It's no good fixing my attention precisely on what I'm doing: I can't move my right arm, which has gone stiff. My ears are ringing, my nose bleeding. My right hand loses sensation for a brief moment, then starts to tingle; I look at it helplessly; it's not obeying me. A cold sweat runs down my back. I breathe slowly and force myself to think, "Move your fingers, move your fingers, Solène, and don't stop moving your hand." Slowly but surely, movement returns. I turn the handle and enter the study. The door slams violently behind me.

The ground is strewn with shards of glass. The numerical boxes, the frames, the collected objects, the files... everything has been torn from the furniture and walls, broken and scattered on the ground. The storm has been especially ferocious here, and even though the wind is now calmer, here and there it continues to shake the torn curtains and blow sheets of paper about, as well as twigs and leaves that the tornado tossed in here through the broken windowpanes.

My father is sitting on the rug in front of his desk, legs splayed out. He reaches an arm out towards me, and articulates painfully, "So-lène... So-lène..." I want to rush into his arms, but remain rooted to the spot. I call him in turn; he doesn't hear me, and now I'm the one who can't hear him anymore; our voices are drowned by a stew of raucous cries and groans.

Suddenly my father's right foot disappears into his shadow; he tries to free his left leg by lifting it with his right hand, but the hand is swallowed by the shadow. He looks at me pleadingly; his face has become dark grey. He begs for help, but I'm incapable of moving.

The walls and floor shake; then the wind dies down, night falls at last, and silence reigns. I manage to move my legs, stand up in one motion, and hurry into the hallway to look for help.

In my parents' bedroom, I see my mother swaying between her bed and the wardrobe mirror; she's in her dressing gown, her hair a mess; she's spinning around like a poor top. At that instant, a wind of mangle-words sweeps in through the broken window in the room, hurls my mother to the ground, knocks me over, and I...

◆

What happened? My hair is full of blood. Why am I stretched out on the landing beside the stairwell? Did I faint in my parents' room? How did I get here? I see Mother at the bottom of the stairs. She's limping, a dishtowel in her hand. She's wearing a kitchen apron over her dressing gown. Her arms and face are covered in grey bruises. She smiles, and announces to the world in general, "Time to eat, children! Come quickly, the soup's hot!"

I get up painfully, and murmur, "Yes, Mother." I've got to tell my brothers. I go carefully through the hallway, avoiding all the shadows. I hear noise in the bathroom; I open the door. Nik and Rob are slumped on the tiles. Nik is sitting on the ground against the bathtub, head hanging down, mouth open. Rob is sprawled face down on the floor. They're both naked, as if coming out of the bath. Nik is holding a wet bathrobe in his left hand, Rob a dry towel against his cheek. Both are barely moving. Their bodies are covered with numerous grey patches. I can't see Nik's eyes, which are turned toward the sink; Rob's fasten on me without blinking. The bathtub is overflowing with earthy grey water; it's spreading across the ground and reaching the first floorboards in the hallway.

With all my strength, I call for Mother's help. She limps to us as quickly as she can, sees my brothers, rushes to them and groans. I help her turn Rob's body over and prop him up on the floor. He's too heavy for us to stand him up completely. I slip on the wet tiles, and Rob falls on his side, stammering, "Good evening good evening."

Behind us, still seated at the foot of the tub, Nik is shaken by a series of brief spasms. He doesn't see us. His absent look remains fixed on the sink. His left arm goes forward and back, forward and back... His legs are trembling. A big patch of shadow has made a hole in his stomach, and is starting to eat away at the right shoulder. He's vanishing gradually before our eyes. Frightened, we let go of his hands. Soon, nothing is left except a foot, a shoulder, and a bit of the pelvis whose pink-grey flesh becomes blurry.

The awful wind returns. Night has come, but calms nothing. Bundles of tattered words mingle with the lethal shadows. A blast of wind pins me like an insect against the hallway partition, just opposite the bathroom door. Mother reaches her arms out towards me, unable to move forward.

The light bulbs, which we'd thought were burnt out, come back on several times, sputtering. I've lost the song, lost the name of the star. I cry *pity* and look out through the wrecked skylight at the distant sky illumined by the full moon. I wait for a sign saying that it's over, that we're saved... A word rushes up in my throat and to my lips: *Lam... lim... lumi...*

Once again, the wind dies down. My body comes gently back down the wall to the ground. Mother gets back up, and together we run to my room, calling out to Ludo. He comes toward us, wrapped up warmly in my blue blanket, and rubs his eyes, as if he'd just woken up.

"Is it time? I can come down for breakfast?"

"Of course, my darling," Mother replies. She turns her head toward our bathroom and calls Nik and Rob. She moves forward in the dim light, enters the room, and pulls Nik's arm toward her; the rest of the body has been eaten by the shadows. Screaming, she lets go of the arm and comes to cling to me, then moves away, takes off her shoes, and makes a few dance steps.

Ludo lets the blue blanket drop and stands pluckily before me, both his arms at his side. "I don't know what's happening to us, Solène, but I'm so frightened..." I kiss him, but he immediately pushes me away in order to finish what he was saying. "Hurry, Solène! Do something! Call Grandpa Welldigger, or else your Mintaka... Or else say a tremendous word... I don't know... Anyway, I'm shutting my eyes. Tell me when I can open them again!"

Mother stops dancing, out of breath. She looks at us strangely... She puts a hand up over her eyes like a visor, as if we were far away. At last she appears to recognize us. "Oh, my dears, where have you come from? How sweet you are!" She comes forward, smiling, takes me by the hand, and leads me to Ludo, asking him to open his eyes and then to go behind her and grasp the cord of her dressing gown with his two little hands; she asks me to do the same behind Ludo, to grasp the cord of his pajamas. This way, we form a line of three. "We're going to dance the ribambella, my darlings, while we wait for your father and your brothers to come back. Ready? Here we go!"

She sings *Gillyflower, gillyflower*, moves her right foot forward and spreads her elbows, marks two beats with the same foot, moves the other foot forward duck-like, marks two beats with the left foot, emphasizing the rhythm with her elbows, which she spreads and brings back to her chest while keeping time. "Come on, children, just like me. Gillyflower, gillyflower... one, two, three... *awasamawasill*, and *pop*! Let's start over..."

I drop out after three rounds of the ribambella. Ludo keeps going, mechanically. He trips over his mother's heels, comes to a stop, and asks tearfully, "Where are Daddy, Nik and Rob?" Mother doesn't answer, and keeps dancing; two beats to the right, two beats to the left. One, two, three, "gillyflower, gillyflower! *awasamawasill*, and *pop*!" She dances like we used to do every year, if I remember right, at the spring festival in Lyon, before the exodus. "One, two, three, gillyflower, gillyflower!... Sing, Ludo dear, sing, my darling! Where did you go, Solène?"

I cover my ears and run into my room. I go to the window and look at the full moon, free of clouds. It's shining with such brilliance that it hides the stars around it. The wind is gone, and so are the mangle-words. I try to remember what could possibly have happened before the beginning of the night, and manage to recall a few things in patches:

We mustn't be afraid
We'd like to tell you that
We were thinking that
Say yes, say yes
Let's go into the *white room*
We'd like to tell you that
We mustn't be afraid

All the while, Mother is still leading poor Ludo in the ribambella. He's stumbling, but gripping as hard as he can onto the dressing gown cord, and repeating in a voice choked by sobs, "Solène, come quick! I can't stand it anymore..." Mother carries on with her dance, then all of a sudden breaks free from Ludo, switches refrains, and beats her foot angrily to emphasize each syllable:

you/ your/ you/ yours
he/ she/ his/ her
our/ your/ their... and... *pop!*

I plug my ears, and repeat as fast as I can:

We mustn't be afraid
We wanted to tell you that
Lam... lim... lumi...
Say yes, say yes

Ludo comes over to me by the window and hides his face in my nightdress. His hair is soaked with sweat. He clings to me tightly and murmurs, "Solène, do something! Call on your secret... Protect me..."

I hear the sound of a fall on the floor below. I take Ludo by the hand and lead him to our parents' bedroom. There, we find Mother kneeling before the wardrobe mirror; she's speaking to her reflection, and perhaps to other images that we don't see. "Come on, little ones, Nik, Rob, Solène, Ludo, come on! And you as well, my little lumin, my little limacine, my little notalone..."

Mother gets up, runs into the hallway, stops on the landing, rubs her eyes, and announces in a merry voice, "Clear night... supper outside... time to eat, children!... hullaballoo's over... stop that racket... it's that I can't abide... put your coats on... blow out the candles... one two three..."

And our poor mother spins like a top, her arms in the air. Her head sways from side to side. Finally she closes her eyes, lowers her arms, and presses her hands to her breast. I hear a rumbling in the distance. The rumbling is getting closer.

The whole house is shaking. The mangle-words stream in through the broken skylight. Mother falls on the landing. A blurred and sticky shadow catches her legs, and climbs slowly toward her head... I cover Ludo's eyes and ask him to repeat after me:

We mustn't be afraid
We'd like to tell you that
We were thinking that
Going into the *white room*

A freezing current of air brushes against us. Ludo and I run very fast back to our room. Ludo is moaning, and I can't find the words to soothe him. A few broken phrases are jostling in my head:

> he us in they say
> us not us us frightened
> neither nor not soul taken
> yes two games that seeing
> must you song the yes
> it's the white cat it's ha!
> not frightened white shadow
> frightened us no not name

We fall asleep in each other's arms, exhausted, wrapped in the blue blanket. The wordless music is here in our heads, *fa do sol la mi la*. It erases the fear and replaces all our dreams.

✦

I open one eye. The sun is shining. We've slept a long time; Ludo watches me while devouring dried fruit that we'd forgotten in the toy chest. He says, "Let's share," and shoves hazelnuts and cisella seeds into my mouth.

Two giddy moths are bumping against the mirror in the room. I look around us; the furniture is on its side, the clothes scattered, the frames broken, the toys spread everywhere.

The walls are still vibrating; I can hear feeble cries, a few groans, and some whisperings, but the storm of mangle-words seems to be over. Has it moved to the south, toward other houses, other families? Are the lethal shadows going to destroy everything in the Borders? My left hand is stricken; so is Ludo's right cheek. If we don't want to be gnawed away by these horrors, we have to act fast!

"Let's get up, Ludo, there's not a moment to lose!"

"Where are Mother, Daddy, Nik and Rob?"

"Please, Ludo, don't think about it now, hurry up!"

"Solène, I'm tired of all your games! I want to find Mother and Daddy!"

"Come quickly! Give me your hand..."

We run into the hallway and down the stairs. When we get to the bottom, I can see the front door standing open a crack. A light wind is blowing it; it's creaking. In the entryway, the daylight is sweeping right over the black-and-white checkered floor. On the tiles, I see the shadow of a body stretched out, an arm reaching forward. A shadow, but without a body.

Bits of phrases are swirling in the air: "Come on children... no but I can assure you that... tax tax taxon... now Solène do you understand... come on children... the game's over..." It's the voice of my father, weak and quavering... I suppose my poor father has managed to move with the last of his strength, that he's crawled from his desk to the stairs, then from the stairs to the entryway, to escape the shadows...

At the sound of his voice, Ludo springs up, bursts into tears, and pleads with our parents to come to our rescue. I tell him to close his eyes and not to let go of my hand. I guide him, preventing him going too far forward on the tiles, so that he doesn't walk on the shadow lying there in front of us.

Ludo clings to me. We hug the wall along the stairwell to the front door; then I have only to make a movement to close the door. Now we're walking backwards toward the banister, and turning left underneath the stairwell. Concealed there is a varnished wooden door, the one to the storage cupboard where my mother hides the key to the *white room*. I open the cupboard, take the key, and pocket it right away so as not to lose it.

"Come on, Ludo, go ahead of me! We're going back up the stairs. No need to be frightened, I'm right behind you. Can you feel my hand there on your shoulder? Now, you can open your eyes. There... Let's go gently forward, but above all, don't look back!"

"Where do you want to go? Do you think our parents are in the garden? I dreamed that Mother was sick. Tell me, Solène, is it true, or was it a dream? Tell me where we're going!"

"Hush! You'll soon see."

On the top-floor landing at the left, we take the gloomy little staircase without a banister, leading to the attic. This time I go first, and Ludo hangs on to my clothes. I pull the latch on the attic door. Here we are in a narrow hallway that has a musty smell of dry grass. On our left is a storage room with latticed windows; to the right is the door to the *white room*, where none of us children has ever gone.

Ludo keeps behind me. He's sweating. He coughs; I can feel his breath on my neck. Now and then he grips my shoulder or my arm; I reassure him as best I can with a gentle word. We're standing before the door to the *white room*.

Suddenly, the whole house shudders. The awful mangle-winds have come back, sweeping over the hill of Poleymieux. Vile rumblings come through the walls and reach us in deformed clusters of sound that get more and more deafening. None of the words is recognizable.

"I want to sleep," complains Ludo. I give him a kiss and hum quietly to him, *fa do sol la mi la*. Between hiccups, Ludo takes up my song. He sings off key, but it doesn't matter. I think: Mintaka. I stop singing and listen to my little brother.

I prepare to put the key in the lock, but then I notice that the door is already open slightly, as if someone had come before us. I think to myself that Mother must have come up before the storm, and that she forgot to close the door behind her...

Gently, I push the door open without making a noise. We're in the doorway, not moving, holding our breath. I'm surprised by a smell of vervain and moist earth, as if we were in the garden...

The entire room is covered in white – a pure, snowy white. I close the door behind us. The walls are no longer shaking. The ground is colored with a white lacquer, as are the door, the baseboards, and the one window frame facing us. The ceiling is white, too. The room has nothing especially marvelous about it, and I wonder why my parents – or else the people who were in the Borders before us, before the exodus – devoted so much care to the upkeep of this space.

Across from us, I see a window that's narrow but tall, like a door. From the fixed crossbar up to the rail, there's just the one glazed panel. It contains a stained-glass window more or less identical to the one in the entryway on the ground floor; this window is comprised of alternating diamonds of white glass. In the center are a yellow crown and an orange disc.

Now the rays of sunlight are touching the lower part of the window. A strange milky light fills the space of the room. I look at Ludo, then at my hands; the same milky white envelops us and bathes us. On our arms we can hardly see the grey marks made by the shadows.

Silence has returned. No more groans or crushed phrases, no more gurglings in the walls. This beautiful silence resembles the new light that now enfolds us; a white silence, shining like pearl. "Look, Ludo, see how beautiful the window is!" He sighs, and asks me worriedly, "Where are Nik and Rob and Mother and Daddy? Why aren't you calling them? We said... all together..."

To the left of the window, under a slanting alcove, I see a chest and a child's cradle. We go closer. The chest is full of baby clothes that look like they've never been worn. I bend over the cradle. It's empty, and the lace sheets and white linen blanket seem never to have been unmade. And yet I know that my mother would come here early in the morning, that she would move things around in the *white room*, with infinite precaution. I could hear her sighing; I could imagine the tender words she spoke. I could hear pattering, rustling, which always made me think she was protecting a being whose survival required constant and attentive care, away from outside eyes.

Nothing, nobody in this little cradle. I slide my hands under the lace sheets, between the sheets and the blanket, under the mattress, under the folds and the seams, under the facing of silk and white muslin in which the crib and its bar are wrapped. Nothing, nobody. But the smell of earth and vervain that greeted us when we entered is here, stronger still on the fabric.

Ludo has sat down in the middle of the room; yawning, he says, "Come on, Solène, let's go. I'm bored. I'm hungry and thirsty. You can see there isn't anyone here..."

All of a sudden, under the cradle I notice an oblong form, whitish and indistinct, transparent like tulle. I bend down to touch it, but this mere movement to get nearer is enough to pierce the strange lace, gathered and transparent, similar to a cicada nymph, that hems a small round mouth... However, the outline of the form, veined with grey, is supple and firm.

"Ludo, come see, quickly!"

My brother turns around and points to the form. "Solène, it looks like a cicada thingy – you know, when they lose their skin... But a giant cicada!" He spreads his arms slightly to illustrate the massive insect he's envisioned.

"It's not a thingy, Ludo, it's a chrysalis..."

"What's a chrysalis?"

"A shed skin, like snakes."

"A snake? Let's get out quick!"

"No, Ludo, no snakes, no cicadas – but something that belongs to someone..."

"Who is it, then? Tell me!"

The rays of the sun have shifted toward the center of the stained-glass window. One ray makes a long, orange-yellow oval pattern on the floor of the room. The color gets brighter and brighter, so bright that the *white room* becomes golden.

I stand near the window and bend over the patch of gold. My hands caress the ray of light. I pour it from one hand into the other, unhurriedly, for a long time. "*Lam... lim...* limenlight! Come on, my little limenlight... gently, now... gently." I wait till the moment when daylight leaves the window and withdraws to go elsewhere. Then I stand up, the palm of my right hand covering that of my left; my hands are a cradle where I hide my treasure. I press both my hands to my chest; I go with small steps toward the door.

"Ludo, open the door! You can see my hands are full..."

"Solène, what are you hiding in your hands? Tell me!"

"Hush now! Get behind me and hold onto my shoulders. Let's go slow. Above all, no sudden movements!"

"Cut it out, Solène! I can see you're not holding anything. Why don't you give me your hand instead!"

"Go on, Ludo dear. You can sing along with me, *fa do sol la mi la*, sing!"

"Sing if you want to, Solène, but I've had enough, I'm not singing! Swear there isn't a snake!"

"I swear on the head of Mintaka."

◆

As we leave the attic, I tell Ludo, "Above all, pay no attention to the voices if they come back in the stairway or the hall. Cover your ears, and don't move away from me an inch!" He stays close behind me, and we go forward slowly. I protect the limenlight in the hollow of my hands. "Don't trip, Ludo! You can see I can't give you my hand!"

In the stairway, the broken voices of Daddy, Mother, Nik and Rob blend together, horribly deformed: "I forbid you... time to eat... I swear to you... let's go... yes children... it's time... you've asked for it... suppertime children... pick up your things... we'd like to tell you that... he bit me... it's time... toward the ruins... time to eat... not be afraid... say yes... you've asked for it... who wants to play... come on children..."

Ludo cries out and presses against my back. I bring my clasped hands to my lips and speak very softly. *"Lum... lumi...* limenlight, my little notalone! My name is Solène, and this is Ludo. Stay with us, don't go away..."

We go through the entryway, making sure not to step on the shadows embedded in the tiles. Here we are now on the front steps, barefoot. The evil noises swirl inside the house, but outside everything's calm, at least for the moment. The sun is shining; birds are singing. We cross the gravel path, then the big meadow. With one hand Ludo pulls up his pajama bottom, which is slipping, and holds onto me with the other, either to the cord of my nightdress or to my right shoulder. He snivels and calls for Mother. I reassure him as best I can, but we have to keep going; I know that if the shadows gain further ground, there won't be any more Solène, or any more Ludo – nobody to call nobody to rescue nobody...

"Solène, I'm frightened!"

"Don't think about it, Ludo, keep looking straight ahead!" I hum *fa do sol la mi la.* He tries to sing along with me, mixes up the notes, sniffles and coughs, but stops crying. We go through the grass, which is still wet with rain. Here and there, we have to step around branches brought down by the storm.

A few feet from the tall trees, music resonates in the air. I stop singing. Ludo stops as well, and looks all around us.

"Who's singing, Solène? Where's that coming from?"

I don't answer, and press my two hands to my stomach. "My tiny one, my light-flower..."

"Cut out the game, Solène! You don't have anything in your hands! It's a trick! It's not your little nothing that's doing the singing!"

Fa do sol la mi la... fa do sol la mi la... The music goes through us and makes the whole space vibrate. I feel light, like dancing.

"It's really beautiful, Solène, honestly, but I've had enough, I'm so hungry!"

"Remember the sugary white flowers at the edge of the great lake, in Grandpa Welldigger's country!"

"OK, but if I think about that it'll be even worse! I'm so hungry!"

Here we are among the thickets, near the hut and the tall trees. Three branches of my copper beech have broken off. The brambles and nettles are everywhere; they sting me, but curiously enough, I don't feel it. The music of air and light makes our heads spin, like a strong liqueur. The sun is at its height. It feels to me as though we've taken hours and hours to cross the meadow, unless time has slowed down...

The mauve-white glow that was adorning the treetops when we were just about in the middle of the big meadow has given way to a blinding yellow light; the soft green of the wet leaves brightens. The heat rises; the grass is steaming. There isn't a breath of wind. A few frayed clouds drag listlessly through the sky. Faraway, toward the mountains in the east, I can make out black clouds, heavy and still. The music has disappeared. It feels like there's no longer any point in singing. For that matter, I'm too tired.

Ludo has let go of my cord and my shoulder. He rubs his numbed hands, and sits on the ground at the foot of the beech tree. "Ludo, do you remember the caterpillar?" He doesn't answer. He's already asleep, his head in my lap. I bend over him; I kiss his hair, which smells of foxes and cumin.

✦

I'm at the foot of the beech tree. Ludo rubs his eyes and removes the thorns and bits of moss clinging to his pajamas; he sits down next to me. We look at the Borders.

The lethal shadows have caused a lot of damage. The left corner of the house, from the parents' bedroom to the kitchen window, has crumbled like any old biscuit. White dust is spreading below onto the gravel and the flowerbeds. A broken pipe is coughing spurts of dirty water. The roof has caved in in two places; the brick chimney has collapsed. Ludo sighs, his head resting on my shoulder. A strange thought crosses my mind: "If this continues, too bad, I don't care, I'll sleep forever..." Two red ants climb onto my leg. Where are my bees? Are they afraid of the storm?

The day is breaking. Some windowpanes of the Borders, cracked or broken, reflect glints of orange light. I can hear a sinister cracking sound. It's coming from the loft. A shower of sparks flies out the window of my father's study. Something is collapsing inside the house. Another shower of sparks shoots out of the living room window. Suddenly I see a wispy grey patch on the side of the house, level with the bathroom window on the top floor. The patch swells and climbs toward the gutter and the edge of the roof. There, it coils up, runs along the gutter, darkens and grows. Yellow flashes streak across it. I can hear sharp sounds, cracklings.

The black mass becomes a cloud, climbs the slanted roof, and splits into three columns of smoke. The windowpanes of the loft shatter, followed by those of the *white room*. Long yellow flames lick the roof. A thought stronger than me decrees, "Do nothing! Above all, say nothing! Wait as long as it takes... *fa do sol la mi la...*" Fascinated, Ludo watches the flames, and looks at his grey hand and the grey patch that's extended the length of his right leg. He's trembling with hunger and fatigue, but doesn't cry.

Even if I wanted to get up to approach the house, to call for help from goodness knows whom... I couldn't. I look at the Borders, and am incapable of moving my head this way or that. My neck and limbs are paralyzed.

The flames have overwhelmed the entire house. They're roaring through the hallways, shooting out the windows, howling in the kitchen and the living room. The fire is devouring the façade. Arrows of fire streak through the waves of smoke. Shutters come crashing down and splinter, their fall causing showers of sparks. Inside the house, doors and walls are coming down; objects are exploding.

Where is my light-child? I'm unable to sing; my tongue and lips can't move. The song has gone out of my head. Explosions! Crashes! Crackling! The flames leap delightedly; they're all that can be heard.

But a very gentle wind is rising. It whistles... one, two notes... dies down, blows like a foghorn... dies down once more, and comes back with a shriller whistle, sounding three notes. The song of the wind and the din of the fire vie with one another. The whistled song of the wind rises: *fa do sol la mi la... fa do sol la mi la...* No! No! The fire roars, the wind stops. A mighty gust, blowing against the fire, flattens the smoke and flames to the ground, and lifts up bundles of lifeless words: *Carn... carn... carn... ideo... morpho... carn, carn!*

The gentle wind returns, insistent. Oh! The wind carries a ritornello; it sounds like the tune of a merry-go-round... *fa do sol la mi la...* then the music ceases abruptly. The flames are roaring, stones are falling. The ritornello picks up again, but further away, over there, quavering, dissonant, as if a music box had just fallen into the inferno.

At the back of the house, the red cedars catch fire like torches. The blaze has taken hold of everything in the villa. Now it begins to calm down. The smoke flattens out, muddled and greyish, or trails in tatters over the charred stones of the façade. Broken beams and lintels glow red. A bitter smell spreads through the garden. White dust and bits of cinder swirl above the big meadow and come to rest on the grass at our feet. Ludo's fallen asleep.

A gust of wind returns and batters the ruined house. Cries and muffled laughs mingle with the crackling of wood and embers. A section of wall comes crashing down, freeing an immense commotion of broken voices: *Come on children... say the name... the lark warbles... clocks destroyed... mother staggers... the bees stick together... the sky is overcast... kiss... you're burning... chinese portraits... do you want to be the death of your mother?... smell of skewers... of fear... the storm is threatening... i'll be you'll be... the keyhole... without touching... corner of the eye... a child... game of patience... someone rang... the shadow stretches... six birds at nighttime... celestial vault... yesterday and tomorrow... a baby... spins in a circle... the cantata... blind man's buff... the scarraged... new city... europe world... are you asleep children?... the sky in the lake... houses of snow... constellation... my secrets... the moth... tricks... fireflies... like rats... the crisis... cats boas and rats... give a name... headlong speed... anthill... headlong speed... mandibles... deathward you go... a little cry... skipping... sidelong glance... the mirometer... without a name... empty screen... no one... a way out... without stars... deep blue... the ferals... falling nowhere... sleeping body... in the mirror... the parents... two voices... alive... white room... on the page... tit for tat... lightning... mountain... in your future... the façade... too young... fading light... cerberus nails... stones... light switched on... mayfly wings... you've asked for it... the white room... notalone... a hand... his hair... gust... erased... no rescue... my little ones... our your their... knock on the door... the key... ray of gold... nothing and no one... the song... cover your ears... windows... smoke... fire...*

The music has disappeared. The old words rise above the ashes, like the hubbub of a tightly packed crowd. But no one is there, nothing but embers, smoke, and bits of words pierced by large black holes. The Borders no longer exists. I don't have the heart to sing.

✦

The last of the flames intertwine, fall, rise again, and falter. In the side of the house that's been ripped open, I see a dark spiral: it's the stairwell, at the top of which a bit of the landing wobbles. A violent shaking demolishes this fragile edifice of embers, which tumbles down, leaving nothing but a gaping black hole.

A new onslaught of flames goes through the rubble from top to bottom, causing the collapse of a section of wall and a zinc gable. A loft window, suspended over the void, tilts slowly, then falls on the gravel.

Smoking debris is piled up on the front steps; the heavy front door, off its hinges and supported by the balusters, burns slowly. The surrounding area has been devastated by the fire: the hedges, the woodpile, the shed, the copses, some of the branches of the magnolia tree, the garden chairs, and the flower bank. Perhaps the fire, fed by the wind, is currently spreading to the neighboring houses... if they still exist, and if the lethal shadows haven't devastated them.

The Borders, a protected zone? It's over. The starving beasts – rats, cats, ferals, hyenas, and all kinds of mutants – are coming in at the back of the grounds, where the outer wall has just collapsed. They're beginning to prowl about the ruins, hoping to find some sustenance. I can clearly hear the rumblings that foretell the coming of the Scarraged or the Ashen. They'll soon have found us... unless the shadows kill us first.

The ruins smoke and crackle. The beasts among the ashes go forward and retreat again, singeing their paws and snouts; they squeal, mew, and roar, but keep on scouring. I can tell they're looking for the cellar entrance; the fire may not have destroyed our meager supplies; the heat of the blaze will have cooked and recooked the dried meats, the glebas, the roots, the preserves, and the emergency biscuits... The beasts can smell it, and jostle with each other to reach the feast, the aroma of which is driving them crazy. Some of them begin to devour each other. Others sink in tatters onto the gravel, brought low by the shadows that are advancing again without waiting for nightfall.

Ludo, exhausted, sleeps with his head in my lap. His left foot is damaged by a shadow. I've lost three fingers of my left hand. It doesn't hurt, but how to react? I should move on elsewhere, to the garden, a better-protected spot, while waiting for... I don't know what.

Waiting for whom? Where's my little notalone? Where's the music? What music? Hey!... is anyone there? Answer... Can anyone hear? Do you hear me? Mintaka Mintaka... what's that name? Who spoke? Answer, I beg you!

My head is going to burst; it's full of frightful cracklings whose meaning I can't understand; Ludo's in a dreamless sleep; he's calm, smiling. He's in luck. But what will become of us? There's no longer any human word in the zone of the Borders; only the growling of beasts, the migraines of mutants, and tatters of ruined thoughts; the Scarraged aren't far off, they're limping towards us, exhausted, drunk with pain, tortured by hunger, but no less ferocious than ever... They're approaching the grounds. I think there are many of them. They're coming. Help! Quickly!

✦

Who cried out? Ludo wakes and looks at me, yawning. "I'm hungry and thirsty. Can we go back to the house now, Solène?" I look at my brother. His left leg is disintegrating bit by bit. He wants to lift a hand to stroke my face, but the blackish little finger breaks off and falls on my dress. His eyes have turned beige, as if there were opaque spots where the corneas had been. I think he no longer sees me. And for my part, I watch him without crying, already knowing what awaits me... I kiss his eyelids, as if a kiss could stave off death... His misshapen mouth calls to me, moaning.

He leans on my shoulder; I don't dare hold him in my arms. I'm afraid of hastening his death by moving too briskly. I see his beautiful lips move; his cheeks are already earthy. I pass my hand delicately through his hair, but a few tufts remain stuck to the skin of my fingers.

I'd like to die in his place... not to see his poor mouth contort every which way to pronounce my name, without being able to; not to hear his groans anymore, feeble like a squeaking mouse. Death is in too much of a hurry.

Suddenly I think of the rabbit kit we buried together, and the cat eaten by the ants. Infected by the lethal shadows, we won't even be those cadavers that rot slowly before disappearing, mingled with the earth. The death from the shadows has no smell, and nothing slow about it; it acts quickly while we're still alive, to reduce us to pieces bit by bit. This way it forces us, alive and without pain, to look at the dust that our flesh and bones become. It wants nothing; it gnaws us, then that's it.

I look at my left hand: the index finger, the middle finger and the ring finger have dropped off; my palm is leaden grey. The first phalanx of my thumb is disintegrating slowly; the nail is coming away, the skin is cracking; at the edge of the cracks I can see pearls of blood that don't have time to flow, for no sooner have they formed than they turn grey and fall away into dust.

Quick, quick! Let the filthy shadows make me a pile of crumbs! The growling of the invaders is getting nearer. I think they're fighting and tearing each other apart to claim our supplies. I don't want Ludo and me to fall into their clutches, even if in the place of our bodies they only found dust and shreds of clothes. I don't want to see them approaching!

Brickebram bracam abraxas! Don't come near! And you, lying sun, evil light, cast your mortal shadows, *abraxas!* And you, stars, fireflies, deceitful bees, *Brickebram bracam abraxas!* Music, dreams, ants, dragonflies, mayflies, *abraxas abraxas!* The very name of Mintaka: *Brickebram bracam abraxas! Lim... lam... lumi...,* three times *abraxas!*

Ah, I want to tear the skin and flesh away from my forehead with my nails or a stone; to scratch all the way down to the bone to remove the filthy little capsule that holds all my thoughts and my words! *Abraxas* on all my thoughts and words! I don't want anyone ever to hear what I've said or thought, and especially not what I'm going to say or think in the little time I've got left! I want to join the dust and the wind where the names of my father, my mother, Nik and Rob are swirling, and soon Ludo's, too!

I want everything to be erased, even the name of Solène. *Brickebram bracam* Solène! *Abraxas* Solène! No more Solène! No more Solène! No more Solène! And when I've removed this worthless little memory, come quickly, you filthy shadows; take me, take everything, now. *Abraxas! Abraxas* on you! I'm screaming against you in silence!

✦

I almost can't see anymore. Or else it's the sun that's setting. My forehead is bleeding. I slashed it with a jagged stone. I'm too weak to attack the bone. It hurts. It's strange, my grey hand and my grey leg feel nothing, and I, Solène, am the one hurting myself with my good hand.

Where did the stone go? I'm so clumsy...

My right eye no longer sees anything. Is it blinded by blood?

Is it the setting sun? My life escaping?... I need a sharp stone to tear out my worthless little memory! Where's the stone?

The trees and ruins are red. The rays of light, the embers, and the shadows on them! Clouds of grey dust swirl in the wind. A form seems to dance on the rubble over there!

Bees are circling in thousands around my tree and the bushes; I can hear them. They've come from all over the land, and their buzzing drowns out the cries of the beasts and the Scarraged.

A column of red ants engulfs my left foot; it doesn't make any difference to me... Soon they won't have anything except bits of dust – too bad for them. My forehead hurts... it's so painful...

Where's the stone? Light rays, embers. The shadows are red.

Where are my parents and brothers? Where's the Borders? I can't turn my head anymore, but I can see things moving around me. The big meadow is covered with grey forms, clinging to one another. These forms seem to be coming out of the earth. I can make out bodies in bunches, grey mounds moving... These bodies have no fear of the lethal shadows; they revel in them, rolling around in them.

There are scraping noises, and the sounds of earth being beaten. The big meadow moves; the forms are shifting the earth, or rolling in the earth and torn-up grasses. Grey hands look for roots and pockets of clay not yet hardened, which some mouths devour greedily.

I can see almost nothing now. The sun is suspended over the crests of the Monts d'Or. Is it finally going to set? It'll soon be night. In my mouth I can taste a few drops of blood.

✦

The heads bent over the big meadow keep chewing and

chewing. Other bodies, standing around the ruins, watch out for anything that could endanger the group. Very agile lookouts surround a few Scarraged ones, catch carnivorous beasts by their paws, and toss them onto the fire.

The grey bodies dig holes and laugh. A crystal-clear laugh, like broken glass; blackish-brown faces chew on clay and raw roots. They don't fear the shadows; they roll around in them like bathers in fresh water. But they don't eat the dead dust that the shadows make; they eat the fresh earth.

Now and then, they stop and gather in a pack, heads and shoulders pressed together. Then from this moving pack there emerges a kind of low murmur that rises like a chant.

Heads lowered... dig holes... creatures' paws... broken glass... Solène! Solène! Blood flows in my mouth; I bring my dead hand to my mouth to wipe the blood from my lips. A grey dust clings to my lips. My tongue licks the dust mingling with the blood in my mouth. I chew on the blood and the dust.

Blood and dust. Whose taste, what taste? Heads lowered... dig holes... creatures' paws... dead hand... whose blood? Oh, Solène! Solène! *Abraxas* on Solène! Shadows, night, swallow me!

✦

I don't see the faces. All their backs are turned. Suddenly, the group in the big meadow stops grazing and turns toward the east, toward the bushes, toward me, so poorly hidden behind the copper beech. They move all together with a single motion, slightly to the right, slightly to the left, to see what the branches are hiding.

Then I can see eyes wide open, shining, unblinking. Those gazes, those yellow glows are observing me attentively. Further away, toward the ruins, lookouts are on the move, and seem to be overcoming the last of the invaders.

The group advances, hesitates, halts. Some change places,

spread out, or come closer together, but none of these grey forms takes their eyes off me. No more murmuring; no more cries or laughs.

The inferno of ruins is no longer crackling. It's almost night. The cicadas fall silent. The only buzzing is that of the bees, whose immense colony crowns the trees and the meadow.

The eyes get nearer. I can smell wax and moist earth. The ants climb up over my face. My paralyzed arms are unable to brush them off. They bite my right cheek where the blood is drying. I'm cold.

The group forms a semicircle around me. I can hear the breathing of those nearest me. Two silhouettes come forward; on their shoulders they carry sacks, or whitish nymphs veined with grey.

The silhouettes move apart from one another to let a small Ashen one through, hardly bigger than a baby. He comes slowly towards me, hands outstretched like someone walking in the dark, and yet he can definitely see me, and doesn't take his eyes off me, for his head moves back and forth in my direction, and he bends over me. I think he's looking at nothing save my poor spoiled face.

His pale grey skin is smooth. He has no hair. The bees approach his head and hands without stinging him. In my own head I can hear his zigzagging thoughts without understanding them.

He bends over me; his little mouth tries to articulate a word I can't hear. In the half-light I can see that he's smiling and trembling. His mouth is drooling slightly. He reaches his right hand straight out toward my face, and one by one removes the ants that were starting to eat me. He strokes my forehead; his hand is warm, soft, slightly damp. Behind him the group looks on without making a noise, perfectly motionless.

All of a sudden, a hiccup shakes the little one's body. Then he trembles violently. Is he shivering? Is he afraid? Does he want to pronounce something very hard to pronounce? I can hear the sound of shattered glass in his body, and this sound spreads behind him, throughout the group of eyes... Are they tremblings of laughter, joy, sorrow? The eyes are unblinking, and the mouths unsmiling, neither happy nor sad. It reminds me of my little Ludo when he listens to me open-mouthed, curious, astonished...

Ludo's head no longer weighs on my shoulder; his whole body has come apart, crumpled on the ground against my dead leg, grey dust. I scream; my head is bursting, but out of my mouth comes only a feeble whistle. I can no longer breathe. I'm suffocating. I'm very cold. My vision blurs. I would desperately like never to see the world again. My eyelids aren't obeying me.

The little Ashen one rests his two warm hands against my cheeks. My skin decomposes and remains stuck to his palms. The little one rubs his hands together to remove the pieces of me; now he comes closer and places his hands once more on my vanished face.

I can hear his thoughts zigzag. Now the mouth articulates, "So... Lène... Solène." I feel like vomiting everything – me... the air... the dust. The mouth has uttered a name, but I think it was me talking in my head.

Hello my little notalone.

My name isn't Solène... *Cicadas... bees... stars... fadosol... lamila... Sol... cic... be... st... cic... cic... cic... I... passes on...*

◆

Anything that dies has had some kind of aim in life, some kind of activity,
which has worn out; but that does not apply to Odradek. Am I to suppose,
then, that he will always be rolling down the stairs, with ends of thread
trailing after him, right before the feet of my children,
and my children's children?

FRANZ KAFKA, *The Cares of a Family Man*, 1917

The education of a child requires that its entire life be engaged.

WALTER BENJAMIN, 1929

The ideal of the shock-engendered experience is the catastrophe.

WALTER BENJAMIN, 1930

◆

Other Titles from Otis Books | Seismicity Editions

Ari Samsky, *The Capricious Critic*
Giovanna Sandri, *only fragments found: selected poems, 1969–1998*
Hélène Sanguinetti, *Hence This Cradle*
Janet Sarbanes, *Army of One*
Severo Sarduy, *Beach Birds*
Adriano Spatola, *The Porthole*
——, *Toward Total Poetry*
Carol Treadwell, *Spots and Trouble Spots*
Paul Vangelisti, *Wholly Falsetto with People Dancing*
Paul Vangelisti & Dennis Phillips, *Mapping Stone*
Allyssa Wolf, *Vaudeville*